SOMETHING EVIL

ALSO BY CAROLINE CRANE

Summer Girl
The Girls Are Missing
Coast of Fear
Wife Found Slain
The Foretelling
The Third Passenger
Trick or Treat
Woman Vanishes

SOMETHING EVIL

Caroline Crane

DODD, MEAD & COMPANY
NEW YORK

Copyright © 1984 by Caroline Crane
All rights reserved
No part of this book may be reproduced in any form
without permission in writing from the publisher.
Published by Dodd, Mead & Company, Inc.
79 Madison Avenue, New York, N.Y. 10016
Distributed in Canada by
McClelland and Stewart Limited, Toronto
Manufactured in the United States of America
Designed by Barbara Chilenskas
First Edition

Library of Congress Cataloging in Publication Data

Crane, Caroline.
    Something evil.

    I. Title.
PS3553.R2695S6   1984   813'.54   84-8171
ISBN 0-396-08419-2

For my editor, Margaret Norton

SOMETHING EVIL

1

SHE had never stepped out on her husband before.

It's only lunch, she reminded herself. Lunch was perfectly harmless. He could have been a business acquaintance, for that matter, except that he wasn't.

They walked down Main Street, looking for a place to eat.

"What would you like?" asked Neale. "Is seafood okay?"

"Seafood's fine." Automatically she drew back as he reached for her hand. She hadn't meant to flinch. Embarrassed, she sought his fingers and lightly wound hers through them. It didn't really count as touching. It wasn't intimate.

"Spanish seafood?" he asked. "With garlic?"

"That's okay."

It was probably all right for the office, but what about later? She imagined arriving at home with garlic on her breath. Solomon would be sure to ask her where she had been. He seemed to resent it whenever she did anything interesting or had any fun without him.

Still, he might not guess that she had been out with a man. And it was only lunch. She wished she could stop feeling guilty.

Neale drew her toward a pink stucco building. It had heavy, carved wooden doors. Aranho's, the sign said. It was Portuguese, not Spanish, but she didn't correct him. He ushered her inside with an attentive courtesy that Solomon rarely showed her. Solomon's mind was usually somewhere else.

It was early, a little before twelve, and the restaurant was not yet crowded. They were shown to a table near the window. Neale asked her what she wanted to drink.

"I have to work this afternoon," Libby said.

"One drink? Don't tell me you can't work after one drink."

She couldn't, but rather than let him think she was unsophisticated, she ordered a Margarita. She had always wanted to try one. Solomon didn't care for sweet mixed drinks and thought she shouldn't either. She had only recently become aware of how controlling he was. She hadn't even known there was a word for what he did when he tried to dictate her tastes, her attitudes, her feelings.

"How long have you been working in that office?" asked Neale. He had interesting eyes. They were blue and very luminous. Soft, instead of sharp like Solomon's. His hair was dark brown and wavy.

"About four months."

"Do you actually sell real estate, or what?"

"Not yet. I just work in the office, but I'm hoping to get my license."

"Is it hard?"

"You have to remember a lot of stuff. You take an exam. I'm working on it." She sipped her water. "What about you? You're a lawyer, right?"

He smiled. "How did you know?"

"Because I've seen you going in and out of that office next to my building. I saw you even before we met in the bank." It had been bold, admitting that she noticed him. She hadn't been able to help it, because of his eyes.

"Oh, *that* office. No, I don't work for them. I was just using their library."

"Where do you work?" She was aghast to think that she might have missed him altogether, if he hadn't been using the library at Barston and Baine.

"I have a legal clinic across town. That's what I call it, a legal clinic. I specialize in criminal cases."

"Is it yours? Your own office?" He seemed young to have his own office. He couldn't have been much more than thirty.

"It's about the only way these days," he admitted. "It's very hard to get into a firm. But it's hard getting going on your own, too."

"I can imagine. How do you get clients?"

"It takes a lot of doing." He sounded vague. She had the impression that he was tired of the subject. He asked, "You don't live around here, do you?"

"Well, not right here. I live in Fairmont Park."

"And you're married?"

She blushed. "Yes, but—"

"That says volumes, that *but*."

The waiter brought their drinks and took their

dinner order. She hoped Neale would forget what they were talking about, but after the waiter left, he continued his questions.

"How long have you been married?"

"Four years."

"And it's not working out the way you hoped."

She wanted to tell him he was the first person she had ever met who seemed to understand her, but she didn't know him well enough to say a thing like that.

Nevertheless, it was true. While there was nothing unspeakably wrong with her marriage, it just wasn't, as Neale said, what she had hoped for. She told herself that her hopes were too romantic, that life just wasn't like that. But she didn't see why it couldn't be. Often she thought she might be better off alone, and then she remembered the loneliness.

Neale asked, "What does he do?"

"My husband? He's a —" She did not know how to explain it. "He's a psychic."

"A what?"

"Well, that's what he does. He has this—he calls it a gift. He can see things. I mean, he really can. He finds things."

Neale's mouth curled in amusement. "What sort of things? Buried treasure?"

"People."

"People?"

"Missing people."

"Do you really believe in that stuff?"

"Of course I do. I've been married to him for four years. I've seen it work. There are quite a few people who can do that sort of thing."

"But that's supernatural," Neale maintained. "I don't believe in the supernatural."

"I don't either, but what he does is not supernatural. It's, well, they call it a sixth sense, and that's really what it is. It's a heightened awareness. He picks up on things. Sort of—I don't know. Emanations. Vibrations. Maybe those things are there for everybody, but most of us don't notice them."

"How well does it work?" Neale was still smiling. "Obviously there are a lot of missing people he hasn't found."

"Of course there are. Any psychic who claims to be a hundred percent infallible is just a phony."

"You sound like a press release."

"I was. I mean, I used to work for a newspaper. That's how I met Solomon. I went to interview him after he broke a famous case where two children were missing."

"He found them?"

"He found their bodies. And he found the killer."

The smile disappeared.

"I remember that," he said. "It was the father, wasn't it? He did it to punish his wife because she left him. He must have been crazy. Anybody who would do a thing like that has got to be crazy."

"You would think so, but they said he was competent to stand trial, and they convicted him. Maybe he should have had you to defend him. At least you'd have pushed for an insanity plea."

"I wasn't practicing then. How do you like your Margarita?"

"It's lovely. Want to try some?" She offered him

the glass. He took a sip and handed it back to her.

"A little too sweet for me," he said.

"That's the way I like it."

He washed down the sweetness with a swallow of his own scotch and soda.

"Does your husband get paid for finding people? Or is that why you have to work?"

"No, he won't take money, just expenses. But he sees people privately. Clients. He gives advice. He writes a column, too. General predictions and things. And he does a call-in radio show. He gets paid for all those things, so we manage. I work because I want to."

"He gives advice? How does he do that? What sort of advice, like a tea-leaf reader?" The smile had come back. She found herself resenting his amusement. It made her feel defensive.

She toyed with her glass. Would Solomon be able to find out that she had done this? Had lunch with Neale?

"He uses psychometry most of the time," she said. "Of course it doesn't work on the radio show, so for that he just has to sense things."

"Psychometry is what?"

"You take an object that's been close to the person physically. A piece of jewelry. Clothing. You can pick up impressions from them."

The smile grew broader. "Well, I'm sorry. I just can't buy it."

"That's okay."

"How do you know it isn't a lot of hogwash?"

"Because I know. So often he's right."

"Anybody can be right a certain percent of the time."

"Well, okay." She was tired of trying to explain it. "Anyhow, you'll get a chance to check him out. He was just called in on another case. The Basile kidnapping. It was in the paper this morning."

"I must have missed it. Certainly hope he finds, uh, whoever it is."

"Why don't we talk about you now?" she asked. "Are you married?"

"Unfortunately, no. Or maybe it's fortunate. What do you think?"

"I guess it would depend on who you were married to. What sort of marriage you had."

"You've got a point there. We can't all be as lucky as Mr. Thayer."

"Solomon."

"Does he appreciate you?"

"Um..." Wavering between the truth and a convenient lie, she was relieved to see the waiter coming with their order. Now they could talk about the food. The appetizer was a varied dish of antipasto. Then there were scallops in green garlic sauce, a tomato and cucumber salad, and chunks of hot, chewy bread.

"This is a real treat," Libby confided. "Usually I just go to the coffee shop for a shrimp salad sandwich."

"You mean you have the same thing every day?"

"Just about. That's what I like."

"You're a creature of habit."

"In some ways, but I told you this is a treat. I

don't miss my shrimp salad sandwich one bit."

"Do you have children?" he asked.

She blushed. "No, I don't."

"You wish you did."

Was he that perceptive? Or perhaps he was tuned in to her, as Solomon, for all his sensitivity to missing children and dead bodies, was not.

"I have stepchildren," she said, "but they're grown up."

"Your husband must be a lot older than you."

"Twenty-two years, to be exact. He looks older, sure, but most of the time I don't even remember our ages."

"Does he have white hair?"

"A little bit of gray. He's not *that* old. He's forty-eight."

"Not what old?"

"To have white hair."

"My mother," said Neale, "had white hair when she was forty."

"Tell me about your family."

"Nothing to tell. They're gone now."

"Where did you grow up?"

"Around. A little bit north of here."

"Where?"

"A little village called Roscoe."

"I know where that is."

"Yes, it's not far from here," he said, "but it's not very conspicuous. Then my mom remarried, and we moved to Trenton. So you see why I don't talk about myself? How are the scallops?"

"Marvelous. I love scallops, but they're so expensive we never have them at home."

She wished she hadn't mentioned home, or "we." It would start him talking about Solomon again.

"Do you live alone?" she asked quickly.

"Yes, why?"

"That was just a question. I didn't mean anything by it." She had to laugh at the situation they were getting into. Neale laughed with her. She didn't want him to think that this was anything more than lunch. She had no other plans or even fantasies. She was not that sort of person.

I'm really not, she told herself.

But she wasn't sure. And she did have fantasies. Ever since that day last week when she had met Neale Janus in line at the bank, she had had fantasies.

2

*T*HE Basile house stood by itself in a wooded area at the end of a dead-end road.

"Good place for a kidnapping," remarked the driver of the police car. "I wouldn't want to leave my kid alone here at night. Even with the leaves off, you can't see it too good from the road."

"Hindsight," replied Detective Mike Tarasco. "We're all smart, after it happens to somebody else. You got anything?" he asked Solomon Thayer, who sat next to him in the back seat.

"Not yet."

They had just arrived, and Solomon's brain was crowded with a jumble of impressions, too many to sort out. There were cars and people. Doors slamming. It was as though he had stumbled onto a party, instead of a kidnapping that was presumed to have been quiet.

Poor kid, he thought. Only a few years ago his own daughter Sybil had been sixteen, Amy Basile's age. He still worried about Sybil, up there in Rochester by herself. He knew what Joseph and Frances Basile were going through.

And the guilt. He could feel their guilt. There must have been something they could have done to protect their child, they would be thinking.

The driveway was circular, looping in front of the house. It seemed a pretentious introduction to a house that was, surprisingly, not very large. The Basiles—unfortunately, as it turned out—had put their money into privacy rather than ostentation. The house was of dull yellow brick, three stories tall, and rather narrow. Its peaked roof and gables gave it an elongated look.

But the driver had been right. The house was secluded even with the trees still bare on that chilly March afternoon.

They started up the flagstone walk, leaving the driver to stay with the car. Mike, the younger and shorter of the two men, was casually dressed in a tan duffel coat and corduroy pants. Solomon wore a sheepskin jacket that Libby had given him. It had become almost a trademark.

Solomon's face, as usual when he started a job, was intent and preoccupied. It was a face made rugged by years of living, although much of that life had been spent indoors. His eyes, a sharp, clear blue, seemed to look directly into people and know what they were thinking, which was often the case. There was a furrow between them as he concentrated on feeling the Basile home.

Mrs. Basile admitted them. She was a thin, quick woman, agitated because there had been mention of the kidnapping in the newspaper that morning.

"We kept it quiet as long as we could," Mike Tarasco explained to her. "You already paid half the ransom and there's still no word. It's time to try something else."

The woman's eyes swept over Solomon. Clearly she did not believe that this "something else" was going to help, but her husband had been ready to try anything.

"It doesn't look good, does it?" she said in a faint voice.

"We don't ever give up," Mike replied. "Not till it's solved. And Mr. Thayer, here, is going to help us. You knew that your husband requested his services, didn't you?"

"Yes. We talked it over."

"Mr. Thayer works with us on an informal basis and without compensation," Mike explained. "And I have to tell you, there's a lot of cases we probably couldn't have broken without his help. Mind if we have a look around?"

Frances Basile didn't speak, but waved a limp hand to indicate that the house was theirs. Solomon understood that she hadn't wanted her husband to call the police in the first place. The fact that the news had gone public seemed, in her eyes, to seal her daughter's doom.

"We'll cover the downstairs first," Mike said, "and then go up to the kid's room. Maybe you can get something there."

"Was anything forced?" asked Solomon.

"No sign of forced entry, but the telephone wires were cut. It was a week ago Wednesday night. The parents went into Manhattan for some kind of business dinner. They always reminded the kid to keep the doors locked. Of course we don't know if she did.

Anyhow, they came home and found her gone. It took a while before they discovered the note on the kitchen table."

"That was it?"

"Yeah. It didn't say much, just that they had her. Next day somebody called his office and asked for five hundred thousand."

"Where's his office?"

"Manhattan. His secretary took it. First she thought it was a joke. Didn't know about the kidnapping. You got anything?"

"Keep quiet, will you?" Solomon stood in the middle of the dining room, his head bowed. It hadn't happened there. It was in the kitchen. She came down for a snack. Down from her room. She had a television there. The door was locked, but they unlocked it. *He.* It was he. One man.

"It was one person. He unlocked the door."

"They said nobody had a key," Mike replied.

"I can't help it. It's a simple lock."

He could see the girl. She had a heart-shaped face and long, dark hair with bangs that were swept to one side.

Long hair. The man liked that. It wasn't only the money. He needed money, but that was not the only reason.

"She could be alive," he said.

"How can you tell?" asked Mike.

"I can't, but he wants her alive, at least for a while."

"Well, sure."

"For himself, not just the ransom. The money was secondary. Spur-of-the-moment."

"Oh." It didn't sound good to Mike.

"Don't say anything to the mother, will you?" asked Solomon. She was not about to believe him anyway, and he didn't care. He had long since outgrown the need to prove himself.

He saw a dark place, underground. A small room or a vault of some kind, and she was in a heap on the floor. She couldn't be alive. The man had kept her for a while, a terrified prisoner. He had collected the ransom from her parents and then thrown her away because she had served her purpose.

"She was just a kid," he blurted, thinking again of Sybil.

"That's right," said Mike.

Solomon told the detective what he had seen.

Mike was baffled. "Like a burial vault?"

"I don't think so. It's just a bare room."

"Whereabouts?"

"I don't have that."

"Can you get it?"

"I'd have to tune into the suspect," Solomon reminded him. They had worked together for years. "And we don't have a suspect."

"Nothing on him?"

"*R*. I see an *R*. He's...different. He seems like one of us, but he's not."

"An alien? Hey, come on."

"There's something dark. Something about him—"

"He's black?"

Solomon snorted impatiently. "I'm talking about inside."

"You mean he's nuts."

"If you want to put it that way. It's not exactly a scientific term."

"Who cares about scientific? Let's find him. Do you want to see the kid's room?"

They went upstairs, but Solomon did not find what he needed in the room. There was a frilly white canopied bed, the mother's influence, and a David Bowie poster. The daughter had begun to assert her own tastes. Had just begun to find herself, to open like a flower, and someone had come along and cut her down.

Mike waited for further information, but the room yielded nothing. It hadn't happened there. Solomon only knew that the parents had come home to find her gone, with the lights and the television still on.

"Let's get out of here," he said.

"Why?"

"It bothers me. I keep thinking of Sybil. I— There was a white cloth over her mouth. Some kind of—maybe chloroform. That's how he got her out. Then he put her in the trunk of his car."

He squeezed his eyes closed, trying to see where the car had gone.

He could only feel her waking in that cold, gritty trunk, slammed about as the car bounced over a dirt road, and her head pillowed on a lug wrench.

"A dirt road," he said. "That figures."

"Man, there's a million dirt roads in the country," said Mike. "Where do we start? Which of the three hundred sixty degrees?"

Solomon couldn't tell him. They went downstairs

and said good-bye to Mrs. Basile. She asked no questions. She hadn't hoped for anything, and Solomon was sure she didn't want to know.

"Do you think it's maybe a mine shaft?" Mike asked as they walked out to the car.

"I have no idea what a mine shaft looks like," Solomon replied. "Why would there be any mines around here, anyway? This is almost New York City."

"Just trying it on for size. We call it brainstorming."

"Maybe I'm wrong."

"Hell, man, you did the best you could. How about a cup of coffee?"

"Later," said Solomon. "I'm going to work on this some more. Why don't you come over tonight? Come for dinner, you and Evelyn."

"What's Libby going to say about that?"

"She likes you. It's okay. I'll start a roast."

He would start the roast when he finished thinking. Mike provided him with a picture of Amy Basile and dropped him off at his house.

Solomon went to his study and sat down at the large oak desk. The study had two casement windows, each with a panel of stained glass at the top. The woodwork was dark, and a dracaena plant stood in front of one window.

It was his dream place, the kind of haven he had always wanted. The dark wood and the stained glass reminded him of something, he was not sure what. Perhaps a house he had visited as a child, or even a church. He couldn't remember. It might have been another lifetime. In any case, it was an atmosphere in which he felt he could reach out and tap the universe, and that was important.

He could thank Jayne, his first wife, for all that he had. It was Jayne who had insisted that he stop fooling around and use his gift to support the family. She had a friend who owned a small nightclub and had gotten him a booking.

Solomon had hated it. He felt that the power was somehow sacred and he shouldn't use it commercially.

Jayne had pulled him off his high horse. It was just a talent like painting or music, she said, and those people used their talents to support themselves, so why shouldn't he?

He never wanted to admit that she was right, but he had made money, and his fame had spread. He went on television and received clients for private readings. He still did that, even though he and Jayne had long since parted company. He charged a fee for the readings, but donated his services to the police. He could not make money from crime victims, or from parents whose children were missing.

He took out the picture of Amy Basile. She must look like her father, he thought. The mother's face was long and sad.

He glanced over at the newspaper shoved aside that morning, but still open to the article on the kidnapping. He hadn't believed that Mike would mention his name to the press. It turned out not to have been Mike, but someone else. Usually the police tried to keep it quiet when they invited in a psychic.

Joseph Basile, the article said, was the founder and president of an importing firm with offices in the Wall Street area of Manhattan. A nice life he had made for himself and his family, but it didn't always help to get too rich. Like carrion, money attracted the vultures.

Poor kid. She was wearing something white, maybe a nightgown. Dragged out of her home. You were supposed to be safe in your own home. Probably the Basiles never considered themselves wealthy enough to warrant a burglar alarm. Should at least have had a dog.

The kidnapper would have gotten the dog, too, the way he got the telephone.

Something dark inside him.

And there were others. He saw it suddenly. He saw frightened eyes above taped mouths. And long hair. All different colors, but always long.

He saw a girl leave a brightly lit store in the twilight. As she walked through the parking lot, a man came out from behind a car. This time there was no chloroform. A handgun instead.

He saw a girl hitchhiking. He saw a car stop. A dark-color car, maybe black. A man driving.

Always the same man. Tall and well built. Solomon strained to see his face, but he couldn't. He was trying too hard. He had to let it come to him.

But he had to see the face. Had to stop the killings. Had to find Amy.

Poor Joseph Basile. It didn't pay to get too rich.

3

THE men were talking about that poor little girl who had been kidnapped. Solomon was on the case now—unofficially, as always. He had seen the house that day. Mike had taken him there, and somehow it ended up with the Tarascos coming for dinner.

Libby had been ready to leave the office when he called to tell her about it. He had started a pot roast, he said, as though that were all that needed doing.

"Thanks," she answered shortly. "You couldn't have waited until the weekend?"

All he had done in reply was breathe, but the way he breathed said it all. It reminded her that she was the one who had insisted upon the outside job.

Before, when she had been his full-time secretary and general assistant, there had been no such thing as a weekend. They worked at home and set their own hours and took whatever time off they wanted. He could not understand what it meant to her to have this job, to feel like a person in her own right, instead of an appendage, an echo of him.

"You wouldn't like it if it were the other way around," she had tried to explain. "If you had to live through me. Why do you think I'm any different?"

For all his psychic powers, sometimes he didn't seem to understand anything about her. Certainly not the fact that after work in the middle of the week, she wanted to relax instead of entertain.

But it was only the Tarascos, whom she knew well. After the first scramble of getting things organized, it was turning into a pleasant evening after all. The Tarascos had brought the dessert, an ice cream pie, which Solomon served while Libby poured the coffee.

"That's the one thing that makes me glad we don't have any money," Evelyn Tarasco was saying. "If I had to worry about the boys all the time—"

"We still have to worry about the boys," Mike pointed out. "There are other things besides kidnapping for ransom."

"So true," Evelyn sighed. "And the bigger they get, the more there is to think of. Would you believe Mike Junior's almost ready for driver training? But it starts off small," she added, lightly touching Libby's arm. "You grow into it along with the kids. I didn't mean to discourage you, in case you're thinking of having a family."

Libby gave her a tight smile. How little Evelyn knew. Having a family was something she thought about all the time. She just didn't seem able to bring it off.

"Libby and I decided not to go that road," Solomon announced. "We had our family long ago, at least I did. We don't see any point in starting all over again. Besides, why add to the population? The world's getting overcrowded as it is."

Smarting at his overbearing attitude, Libby said, "There's such a thing as adopting. That wouldn't add to the population."

"Mike was adopted," Evelyn put in.

Mike smiled. "Only by my stepfather. That doesn't really count."

Libby was silent. It was the first time she had spoken of adoption, or even thought much about it. Putting it into words seemed to crystallize the idea, until it was swept aside by Solomon.

"Why adopt?" he said loftily. "If it doesn't happen, I say leave it alone. There are plenty of other things to think about besides kids. A whole world out there."

Mike looked at Libby. "Is that your feeling, too? After all, they're his kids, and they're grown up now. You never had the experience of raising them."

"Of course she agrees," said Solomon. "We have a full, interesting life together. For people like us, kids would just get in the way."

It's not true, she thought. *We don't have any life together, not anymore.*

He mustn't know how she felt. For all these months, maybe even a year, she had managed to conceal it.

"Evelyn, more coffee?" she asked.

Mike's plump, blond wife held out her cup, and Libby refilled it.

She could not remember when it had started. She

thought it was the time he had flown to Chicago to appear on a television show with another psychic detective. She remembered thinking, *What if something happens? What if the plane goes down?*

It had been a tantalizing thought, and not as guilt-provoking as she might have expected. It wasn't as if she could make it happen.

But if it were to happen, then the problem would be solved. She wouldn't have to ask for a divorce. That, he would never understand. She didn't think he meant to be the way he was. He did it all unconsciously, and she did not want to take conscious revenge. Even though he trampled on her feelings, she still felt protective of his.

But if his plane were to crash...

"Mike, more coffee?"

Solomon's eyes slid toward her. She knew she had been thinking too much. If she couldn't stop, then she must block her thoughts.

It was a trick she had taught herself long ago. A very useful trick for the wife of a man like Solomon.

She pictured a high brick wall. A garden wall. She saw vines climbing up it and felt the sunshine all around her. A sunny garden. It was pleasant on that March night.

"Good pie," she told Evelyn, feeling that something was expected of her. She wondered if Solomon could see her garden wall, and what he would make of it.

"Oh, it's just a store-bought thing," Evelyn protested. "We picked it up at the bakery."

Evelyn took a breath and frowned. Her mind was

not really on the pie. "Don't you think it must have been somebody who knew them personally? After all, they're not *that* rich. And if the door wasn't forced—"

"I don't think so," said Solomon.

"How do you know all that?" Mike asked his wife.

"It was in the paper. And you kept it out for a week. Now that you told the media, does that mean you've given up on her?"

"We never give up."

"Well, what do you really think?"

"About what?" Mike could be annoying with his professional discretion.

"You know! Her chances."

"Why don't you ask Solomon?"

"I'm asking you both," said Evelyn. "I want to know. That poor little girl."

"What we think isn't going to change anything," Mike replied. "But it's five days since the ransom was paid. That's not good. The more time that goes by, the less good it is."

Evelyn turned to Solomon for his opinion.

"It's hard to say." He sounded thoughtful. His vision hadn't been clear, Libby decided.

"And it wasn't..." He paused. Then he said, "There were others."

"What?"

"Others. It wasn't the money."

"What others?" asked Libby.

"Hitchhikers, mostly. This one—the money wasn't primary." He paused, and his eyes took on a faraway look.

"It's hair," he said. "He'll take only the ones with long hair." He glanced at Libby, whose dark red waves fell below her shoulders.

"But that's only one thing. It's not an attraction, it's anger."

"At what?"

"His life. I can feel the rage. There's some terrible thing he thinks happened to him."

"Did it?" asked Mike.

"Hard to tell. If he thinks it did, then for him, it did. It's his reality. It boils up inside him, makes him have to kill over and over again."

Evelyn moaned and set down her cup. "I don't think I want to know anymore."

"I wish I didn't have to," Solomon said.

Libby felt a pang of sympathy. She knew it was a burden for him. More than a burden. Often he could feel the victim's fear and pain. He could feel the death agony.

"I can't understand why girls hitchhike," Evelyn exclaimed. "That kind of thing seems to happen so often. I'm glad I only have boys, so I don't need to worry."

"Don't forget Dean Corll, that guy in Texas," said her husband. "He killed about thirty male hitchhikers. Tortured them, too."

"Do you guys *like* this kind of thing?" Evelyn cried.

"You brought it up. And, no, we don't. I was only trying to emphasize that nobody's immune."

"Okay. I'll guard the boys with my life." She sounded resentful. "There are so many wackos."

"And they're all men," said Libby.

"It's the nature of the sex drive," Solomon told her. "It takes a different turn in women."

"I think it's cultural expectations."

"Nobody expects that sort of thing, Libby."

"All right, then, frustrated cultural expectations."

"You don't know what you're talking about. You only make yourself sound foolish."

She settled into a furious silence. Evelyn glanced at her, and Mike tried to smile reassuringly. They could see through Solomon, but it never made him stop.

Evelyn leaned toward her and whispered, "We have our differences, too. You should have heard the fight we had last week."

Evelyn didn't understand. A fight was not the same thing as a constant chipping away of self-esteem. Libby managed to keep her dignity, because she despised people who fought in front of guests. But as soon as the Tarascos left, she confronted him.

"That wasn't very nice," she said, "to tell me in front of them that I sounded foolish."

"You did, didn't you?"

"I didn't happen to think so. And if you thought so, you could have kept it to yourself or saved it for later. Don't you realize you only make yourself look bad when you put me down all the time?"

"I say what I think." To her ears, there was more than a trace of smugness in the statement. He began to stack the coffee cups and saucers.

"Another thing," she went on, following him out to the kitchen. "What did you mean when you said *we* decided not to have a family? You know I never decided anything like that. It was all your idea."

He set the dishes on the counter and looked at the clock. "Is this going to be a long discussion? Don't you think we ought to clean up first?"

"You can time it if you want to," she replied. "I asked a question. What gives you the right to decide things for both of us?"

Carefully he placed the cups and saucers in the dishwasher, then started back to the dining room for another load.

"Something's bothering you," he said. "I could see that as soon as you came home this afternoon."

Evening. It was evening by the time she came home to be confronted by a houseful of guests. She refrained from mentioning it. He had a way of deflecting arguments, and she would not take his bait.

"What's bothering me," she told him, "is your habit of making a decision and then projecting it onto me. You do that with your own attitudes and feelings, too, instead of ever listening to me."

"I'm listening," he answered as he picked up the place mats. "When do I not listen to you?"

"Always. You make a show of listening, and then you proceed to tell *me* what I'm thinking and feeling. I don't think you really see me as a separate person."

At the sight of a stubborn stiffening in his face, as though a veil were being drawn over it, she cried, "We didn't used to be like this! We could talk to each other. We used to be friends. I don't know what happened."

"You don't know what happened?" he asked.

"You're the one who's been pulling away. What about that silly job thing of yours? Where does that fit in?"

He didn't understand at all.

"And I get the feeling you're holding something back," he went on. "Some area of your life that you don't want me to know about."

"Everybody," she replied, "is entitled to a little privacy, and believe me, I don't have much."

She hurried upstairs to their bedroom. He would not join her until he was ready to sleep. He all but lived in that study of his.

She sat down on the double bed and thought of the night that was coming. So close, in that bed. She couldn't block her thoughts when she was sleeping. Sometimes, in a general way, he even knew what she was dreaming. She did not think she would dream about Neale, not yet, but something would be there, some preoccupation, and Solomon would feel it.

In fact, as he had just stated, he already did. And she had agreed to meet Neale again tomorrow.

She could break the date, stand him up, give him up, but it wouldn't solve the problem, which was between Solomon and herself.

What's the matter with me? she wondered. Why can't I make him understand?

4

AT three o'clock on Thursday morning, Joe and Frances Basile, sleeping in twin beds, woke to the shrilling of the telephone.

"Oh, my God," said Frances.

"I'll take it." Joe was prepared for anything. At that hour, it was sure to be important. He picked up the phone.

A smooth male voice asked, "Mr. Basile? I'm calling about your daughter."

Prickles of ice went down Joe's back. He remembered what they had said about the voice that called at his office with the ransom demand. It had been well modulated with good articulation. An educated voice.

"Yes?" he asked cautiously.

"I thought you might want to know what happened to her." The voice paused.

Joe glanced at Frances. He did not want to say too much.

"Of course I do," he replied.

The voice went on calmly, almost cheerfully. "I'm

sorry to tell you this, Mr. Basile. There was a little problem with the chloroform. You see, we used chloroform to subdue her, to make it easier, you know, and I'm afraid there was some problem with regulating the dosage."

"What are you saying?" Joe's head began to swim and his heart to palpitate.

"I was trying to break it to you gently." The voice had acquired an edge. "What I'm saying is, your daughter's dead, so you can stop worrying. She's dead. She can't feel anything now."

"You're crazy," Joe said hoarsely.

"Maybe I am. I just thought you'd want to know. You don't have to worry about her anymore. Nothing else can happen, am I right?"

"Where—where—" Joe clutched at his chest. Frances moved over to sit on the edge of his bed with her arms around him. Her head rested on his shoulder. He wondered if she could hear what came through the phone.

"I'll tell you," said the voice. "We couldn't leave the evidence around, you know, so we dumped her in a swamp. It was nighttime. Somewhere around the Meadowlands. Around there. You can see a little brook running through the place. Well, I won't keep you, Mr. Basile. You're probably trying to trace the call, but it won't help. I'm at a pay phone. Good night."

There was a click. Joe's hand trembled as he set down the phone. He saw his whole life running past him like a movie. He saw all his hard work. Admittedly, some of it was for the sake of work itself. He loved it. But mostly it was for his family. For Amy. He wanted to give her everything he and Frances never had. He wanted to give her a happy life.

His wife's arms slid away from him. "She's dead, isn't she?"

"That's what he said." Joe could not believe it was his own voice talking. His chest still hurt and he thought he might be dead himself, because he didn't feel that he *was* himself anymore.

Frances pressed her lips together and stared at the floor. She wore a pink brushed nylon nightgown that made her look sixteen. Amy's age.

"Did he say where?"

"No," Joe lied. "I couldn't get that." The police had undoubtedly picked it up. They were monitoring the phone.

He wished she would cry. She couldn't even cry, and neither could he.

"Would you like some coffee?" she asked.

"I don't think I'd better. My chest doesn't feel right."

"Oh, Joe!"

As if it mattered about him. But maybe she cared. She didn't want to be left alone.

"I'm going to call the police," he said. Not that there was anything anybody could or would do until morning. Even if he and Frances drove out to the swamp, they could never find anything in the dark. And maybe they should leave it to the police to find it.

"I guess maybe," he said, "I'll have a drink."

"Should you?"

"I think I should."

Libby woke in the morning before the alarm went off. Solomon lay with his back to her, breathing heavily. Thoughts of yesterday and last night drifted through her mind. Thoughts of Neale, and what Solomon had said about the kidnapping. If he found the girl, even her body, he would be a hero. She respected that. She loved it. But Neale respected *her*, and that was important, too.

She gazed at the stained-glass panel above the window. In the late morning, when she was not there to see it, the sun would spread shattered color all over the floor and wall. It was odd, having that brilliant stained glass in the old, dark house. Solomon considered the house a palace. It was better than the homes either of them had grown up in, but it was not a palace.

She wondered that she had even been able to sleep. She was wide awake now, still thinking of Neale.

Solomon would know. He would read it in her mind. He had suspected something yesterday, but she had managed to block it. She could not keep doing that. Or keep seeing Neale. She would have to be honest with Solomon, but then she would hurt him, and she didn't want that. All she wanted was someone she could talk to, someone who would listen and care about her.

Solomon had been like that once. He had changed under the pressures of work, or perhaps had come to take her for granted.

Or maybe it was her fault. She had been starry-eyed and hero-worshipping when she married him. It was no wonder that he took her for granted. Now they were locked into a pattern that he couldn't see and she could not get out of.

Perhaps, if they had a baby...

She moved next to him and put her arm around him. He stirred and muttered fuzzily. She ran her hand down his side.

"It's almost seven o'clock," she said.

He rolled onto his back. "What are you trying to do?"

"I just want to make love."

His eyes looked into hers. She tried to think love. She thought of their wedding day, a small ceremony in her family's church. She had worn a knee-length white dress. Her parents had thought he was too old for her.

"If you don't want to..."

He pushed aside the covers and reached for her. She could feel the hard muscles of his back under the flannel pajama top. She ran her hand under the pajamas, rubbing his back. They took off their nightclothes and again came together. She must think only love and not let him know how much she wanted a child.

"I love you," she whispered.

"Do you really?"

She put her finger against his mouth. She thought of love. It was thick and golden, like honey. She wondered if he could see honey in his mind, pouring from a jar marked Golden Blossom. What would he think?

It didn't matter. He was not reading her thoughts at all. He was responding, and she let herself move with him.

When it was over, she lay dreamily floating. *This time*, she thought. This time it's got to happen. Please.

She was aware of Solomon resting on his elbow, watching her.

"What's going on?" he asked.

She should not have been thinking. She closed her eyes and saw the honey again.

"I feel so peaceful, I don't want to get up."

"It was your choice."

He was baiting her into another argument about the job. She lay still, not answering, but the honey image had gone and something jangled and discordant took its place.

"It's still my choice." She sat up, put on her nightgown, and went into the bathroom.

Solomon knew there was something wrong, something going on with her, but he could not find out what it was.

She was only being temperamental again, and there was nothing he could do about it. After she left for work, he took *The New York Times* into his study. As soon as he began to read it, the telephone rang.

He picked it up. "Hello, Mike. You got a phone call, didn't you?" He could suddenly see it. Evelyn and little Johnnie in a doctor's office.

"Yeah, uh, two calls," Mike replied.

"A personal one. How's the kid?"

"My kid? Oh, uh, it isn't much. He was horsing

around on the way to school and slipped on a patch of ice. Cut his forehead. They're putting in a couple of stitches. Compared to Basile, we got off easy."

"What about Basile?" He hadn't seen that. Only Mike's son.

"It could be a hoax. Basile got a call from somebody who claimed to be the kidnapper. Told him his daughter's dead. It was an overdose of chloroform during the abduction."

Solomon was silent. And angry. Even knowing she was dead, they had collected the ransom. He could never get used to it. These animals. But that was too good a word for them. The worst kind of animals were people.

"Was it the same voice?" he asked.

"When the guy called that first time, Basile didn't talk to him. They called the office and his secretary got it. Remember, they ripped out the phone at the house."

"Right."

"We've still got to find her, Sol."

"And him."

"There was another call," Mike went on. "Somebody named Iris Knapp. She saw that thing about you in the paper yesterday."

"And?"

"Another kid missing."

"When?"

"A year ago. We didn't have it. She lived in Paterson then. She's alone and it's her only kid, four years old. She doesn't have much hope, but she wants to know."

"Anybody'd want to know," said Solomon. "Okay, I'll give her a call. What's her number?"

Mike gave him the number and Solomon dialed it, still thinking about Amy Basile. At least it had been a quick death, but it didn't jibe with what he had seen. He couldn't understand it.

Iris Knapp had a job with an insurance office. She was in a hurry to get started, and asked if he would meet her after work the next day.

He could already see her, a young, round-faced woman with curly blond hair, wearing a green pantsuit. He saw a black car driving through the woods.

And then he saw water. He saw ripples in the wind, ripples that seemed to blow on forever.

5

SHE had told Neale that she would finish work at five o'clock and that Solomon would be busy preparing for his radio show.

"Great!" Neale had said. "I'll give you a call."

She waited for the call. It never came.

This is it, she thought. It's over.

She was glad it was over, even before it had really started. She knew it had not been the answer to her problems with Solomon. Now she would have to face the situation directly. She would have to talk it over with him.

But she also knew what would happen. He would imply that it was her fault, that she had been stupid or selfish, or both. He would make her feel guilty for not being a good wife. It would work, too. She had been well conditioned to feel guilty.

As Solomon wanted a good wife, her parents had wanted a good daughter. She had tried. She had stifled her naturally exuberant nature and given up the idea of a singing career. Finally she had won their grudging approval, but at a price. The price was her self.

And then she had fallen into the same pattern with Solomon. If she had had her self, she might have been able to handle it better. Or even married someone else, someone who had a little respect for her.

Someone who loved her.

He says he loves me.

But she wasn't sure. He loved her sometimes, when she was being his good little girl. When remnants of her self appeared, he seemed not to love her at all.

Who am I? she wondered. I don't even know who I am.

A client came in and interrupted her reverie. The client was looking for a three-bedroom house in the $25,000 range.

"I'm afraid you won't find anything like that," she told him, "outside of a mobile home."

It was true, but at the sight of his crestfallen face, she wished she hadn't said it. She turned him over to one of the brokers and went to the rest room to repair her makeup.

She felt strangely let down, in spite of her relief about Neale. She was shocked at herself for feeling that way, but she couldn't just go home. Solomon probably wouldn't even be there. He would be out on that kidnapping case.

She left her office and walked past the bank where she had first met Neale. In retrospect, it almost seemed like fate. She had waited in so many bank lines with so many strangers, but this was the first time she had struck up a conversation with anyone. Or responded when someone else started talking to her, which was actually what happened. It was a mutual attraction right from the start.

She tried to think of something to do. If she went home, Solomon would expect her to type his introduction for the show. She remembered reading once that in the early days, typewriters were called typing machines, and the people who operated them were referred to as typewriters. That was exactly the way he treated her when they worked together—like a typewriter, an inanimate device for his convenience, instead of a partner.

Hurrying footsteps pounded the sidewalk in back of her. A voice said, "Hi, how are you?"

"Oh!" she exclaimed, feeling her face turn pink. "I thought you were going to call me."

"Didn't get a chance. I'm glad I found you. Do you feel like some dinner?"

Gallantly he took her arm and led her across the street, not to Aranho's this time, but a place called the Broadway Diner. It had a counter, but in the back there were tables and booths. She liked the booths best of all. They offered a semblance of privacy.

"This is plain old American food," he said as they studied the menu. What he meant was, it was less expensive than Aranho's. She wondered if lasagna was considered American. Probably, by now.

"I think I'll have the club sandwich," she decided.

It came with french fries and cole slaw. "And coffee. Okay?"

"You're sure that's enough? This is dinner."

"It's plenty. Thanks." She wondered if Solomon would have been so concerned about her. Actually, back in their courtship days, he might have. Perhaps it was her fault that he had changed.

After the waitress took their order, Neale leaned forward, resting his arms on the table.

"How's your husband doing on the kidnap case?"

"Oh, I don't know. He just started." She would not repeat the things Solomon had said last night. That was police business, and it might not be accurate anyway. His impressions were not always accurate.

"I'm really interested in knowing more about this," Neale said. "I always thought that kind of stuff was phony. How does he do it? When he's seeing something, for instance, how can he tell if it's the real McCoy or just his imagination?"

"I think it's the quality of the thing," Libby replied. "He says it's like actually seeing it or feeling it. And it just comes to him. When you're imagining something, usually you make some kind of decision as to what you're imagining."

"Not always. Haven't you ever waked up at night, seen your clothes hanging on the door, and imagined it was a person standing over you?"

How horrifying, she thought. "I don't think I ever hung my clothes on the door."

"You must be a very neat person," he said with a

grin. "Or do you hang them on the floor?"

A smile played at her mouth. "I'm compulsive. They go straight into the laundry hamper. Unless they need dry cleaning. Then I make them last a while longer. Now come on, I want to know more about you. What sort of person are you?"

"I'm a fun person," he replied.

"What sort of family did you have? You said your mother remarried. Was it divorce, or what?"

"No, my father died."

"Oh, I'm sorry."

"It's okay. My stepfather was okay."

"Did you have brothers and sisters?"

"One brother. Older. He wasn't around much."

"It must have been lonely for you."

"It was, out in the country. But let's skip that, shall we?"

"I'm sorry. It's none of my business." She was embarrassed at having pried.

"It's not that," he told her. "There's just nothing to say about it."

"About your whole *life*, there's nothing to say?"

"It's been uneventful."

"Well, anyway, they must be proud of how you turned out."

He smiled wryly. "How do you think I turned out?"

"I mean, having a profession, and all that. And I think you're a nice person. You are, aren't you?"

"I get by."

The waitress brought their coffee. Libby stirred in her cream and replayed their first meeting in the bank. They had been next to each other at one of the tables, filling out their deposit slips. Then they had gotten into the line, which was extra long that day because of computer trouble, and he had made some remark about the delay.

She wondered why he had an account at that bank, when his office was across town.

"What are you thinking about?" he asked.

"Oh, uh, about how I wish they'd bring the coffee after dinner instead of before. Whoever heard of coffee as an appetizer?"

"They always do it," he said. "You know, I'm really curious about your husband."

"Yes, you seem to be."

"Does he ever talk to you about his work? I mean, if he's working on a case?"

"Now and then, but not much. Why?"

"I just wondered. Don't you ever want to know? Maybe you don't have any natural curiosity."

"I—"

"I mean, a case like that is big news. I should think you'd want to know what's happening."

"Well, I guess when anything happens, we'll find out," she said.

"Sure, along with everybody else."

She laughed nervously and wondered if perhaps his interest was more in Solomon than herself. "What are you, a reporter looking for a scoop?"

"No. Just a lawyer." He seemed entertained by her doubts. She was glad he thought it was funny and didn't know how insecure she really was.

He went on to explain, "I handle criminal cases,

you see. That's why I'm interested. Does your husband ever work with lawyers, or just the police?"

"Well, sometimes with the prosecutor's office. I think there was one time a criminal lawyer called him, because he really thought his client was innocent." She picked up her cup, blew on the coffee, and tested its temperature.

"Was he?"

"I don't know. It was inconclusive."

"What do you mean? Your husband couldn't find anything?"

"Nothing they could prove, one way or the other."

The waitress returned with her club sandwich and his Salisbury steak. As soon as she left, before Neale could resume his conversation about Solomon, Libby asked, "Were you ever married?"

He looked at her, startled. Then he began to laugh. "What was that for?"

"Well, you know all about me, so why shouldn't I ask? You said you're not married now. I was wondering if you ever were."

"Uh, no."

"Any girl friends?"

He ate his steak in silence. She thought he wasn't going to answer. Then he said, "One. Only one that meant anything. And a lot of one-night stands."

"What happened? Oh, I'm sorry, that's none of my business."

"It's okay. She died."

"Oh, Neale, I *am* sorry."

Again he shrugged. He was no longer affected by it.

"In my house. Not here, it was another place. She—I don't know, it was drugs, or something."

"She O.D.'d?"

"In my house. For a while I thought she killed herself. They did an autopsy. I didn't even know she was on drugs."

"That must have been horrible for you."

"It took me a long time to get over it." He sawed at his steak. She had never seen anyone use a knife on Salisbury steak before.

"It was a long time," he said again, "before I came out of it."

"I can imagine. You must have been terribly shocked as well as sad."

"That's right, I was. Didn't even know what I was doing half the time. I couldn't remember. Used to take long walks and think about her."

"What was her name?"

"Alex. Alexia."

"That's pretty," she said. "Alexia's a pretty name."

"Tell me how this psychometry works."

She tilted her head and glared at him sideways. "You *are* a reporter."

"No, honest, I'm just nosy. I read books on science and occult things. I'm really curious."

"Did you know about my husband before you met me? Is that why we met?"

"Would you believe me if I told you I didn't?"

She thought about it for a moment. "All right, not why we met, but why we started seeing each other. You already knew my name."

"Well, it wasn't that way at all."

She picked up a pickle slice and ate it. If she really thought, for one minute, that he was more interested in Solomon than herself, she would leave.

He reached across the table and put his hand over hers. "Believe me?"

"What choice do I have?"

"Good." He patted her hand. "And the burden of proof isn't on anybody. Now that we've got that settled, will you humor a nosy guy and tell me how it works?"

She sprinkled salt on her french fries. "I'm beginning to doubt you again."

"Okay, I'll bug off."

"Anyway, I already told you. We talked about it before. I said it's from things that were close to the victim or the missing person. Or it could be something from the scene of the crime. If he holds it in his hand, he gets impressions. Mental pictures."

"Yes, you did tell me, but I don't see how it could work. There's no principle to it. Anything that works has a principle."

"Once I read," she began, knowing she was entering a whole new morass of doubts and questions, "that there's been some research on it, and they came up with a theory that the body gives out a kind of energy. They call it biomagnetic energy. They say it leaves an impression on objects close to the body, and that impression stays there indefinitely."

"Impossible."

"Well, I don't know. I'm not a scientist. And they said if there's been some emotional crisis, the impressions are especially strong. I guess they're there for anybody, but only people with the right sensitivity can pick them up."

He began to laugh again. She liked his smile. It was slow and very sexy.

"Okay," he said, "you've convinced me."

"I have?"

"That it's a lot of b.s. And I promise I won't ever bring it up again. What would you like to do after dinner?"

6

WHEN Solomon arrived at the police station, the woman was already waiting. She did not look at all like the image he had seen of her. The blond hair was long and straight, and instead of a green pantsuit, she wore jeans and a tan coat.

He had had enough experience not to be surprised.

"Did you bring anything with you?" he asked when Mike had introduced them. "A photograph, and something belonging to your child?"

"I have it here." She opened a manila envelope and took out an eight-by-ten portrait of a smiling blond child in a miniature football jersey.

"That was the last—" she began. "Just before Christmas, a year ago. They were having a special at the studio. I—"

She stopped, and her face grew taut. Reaching again into the envelope, she brought out a small, blue sock.

"I found it under his bed," she told Solomon, "after he disappeared. He wore it a couple of days before. I just couldn't wash it. I kept it this way."

"That's good. Very good." Solomon held the sock in his clasped hands and relaxed his mind.

"Ritchie," whispered a voice. Richard Knapp, Jr.

A face floated into view. Its eyes were closed. It seemed to be immersed in some kind of substance with a greenish tinge.

Water, he thought. But where?

Without speaking or looking at Mrs. Knapp, he picked up the photograph. The child had been gazing straight into the camera. That was good. He met the boy's eyes. For a moment, they seemed alive.

He saw the beginning of a driveway. A long gravel driveway, full of weeds. Two stone posts flanked the entrance. In front of one was a rusted mailbox. The name on it had flaked away. All that remained was an *ND* and an *L*.

He began to move along the driveway. Soon a house came into view. It was sand colored, faintly reminiscent of the Basile house, but long abandoned. Its windows were boarded, its grounds overgrown with weeds.

A wind blew around it, swaying the bare tree branches. The only thing left of civilization was a lush growth of rhododendron bushes, a row on either side of the front door.

"An abandoned house," he said. "Were there any abandoned houses near you, with posts at the driveway entrance? Posts made of stones stuck together with mortar?"

"N-no," she began, trying to think. "Did you see it?" She bit her lip. Her child could not be in such a place all this time and still be alive.

"I don't know where," he said. "Where in or around the house." Somewhere in water, he wanted to add, but he hadn't the courage to tell her.

He studied the picture again, then closed his eyes. He moved back from the driveway, trying to see where the house might be.

He saw a narrow lane full of potholes. It looked almost as untraveled as the driveway. They would not be able to see the stone posts from any public road. He couldn't get farther back than that.

"I can't figure out where it is," he said. "It may be hidden from the road. There's a tall tree. An elm, I think. You don't find too many elms around anymore. If it were anyplace your child could have walked to, I'm sure you'd know about it."

"Is it a residential house?" she asked. "There was an abandoned warehouse near the river."

Solomon was interested in her mention of the river, but he knew that wasn't right.

"It's definitely a residence," he said. "Much too secluded for a warehouse. Maybe we should try driving around in your old neighborhood and see if we can pick up something."

They went out to his car. He sensed her watching him and sensed a growing admiration in her. A kind of clinging. He was the first person in almost a year whom she had been able to trust. And he knew at once that her husband had left her because he blamed her for the child's disappearance.

As they pulled away from the police station, he

asked, "Did you always wear your hair this way?"

"No," she said, "I let it grow after—everything happened."

"It was short and curly, right?"

"Yes." She looked at him in surprise.

"And you had a green pantsuit."

"Yes. The day Ritchie disappeared. I never wore it again. I spent the whole day—first I looked for him myself. Then I called the police. All *day*. And the next day, and—and after a while they gave it up. I went on trying to find him. But I had to take a job after Dick left, so I only had weekends."

"Dick left because of the child," said Solomon. He saw a face distorted with anger and heard a voice raging about "carelessness," and "You can't even watch your own kid."

"I couldn't—it was only a second. He was in the yard, and then he was gone. I didn't know where to start looking."

"They can go in any direction," he said.

"And they go so fast. It happened once before, in the supermarket, but I found him. I never told Dick about that," she added.

"He shouldn't blame you," said Solomon. "You can't hang onto kids every minute. They'll slip away, or stop to look at something, then they'll lose you and get disoriented and start to wander. And you don't know which direction to begin looking."

"You sound as if you've been there."

"Not quite the same."

"Do you have children?"

"Two. They're grown up now."

She was silent, reflecting on her own child's lost chance to grow up.

Then she said, "The police thought somebody might have taken him right out of our yard, but they never found anything. And nobody saw anything. I wish I'd known about you sooner."

It wouldn't have made any difference, Solomon was sure.

"If I only just knew," she went on. "Even if I knew he was dead, it would be better than this."

"I hope I can help, but I can't promise anything. They told you that, didn't they?"

"Yes, they did."

Iris Knapp and her family had lived on a street of modest homes near a factory district in Paterson. She pointed out the house, a one-story white clapboard with a small, fenced-in yard. Partially visible in back of the house was an umbrella-style clothesline loaded with baby clothes.

Solomon pulled over to the curb and stopped the car, but left the motor running. He studied the house, trying to see what had happened there a year ago. Trying to pick up a trail.

He saw a snowsuited figure leaning against the fence, looking out.

His mind erupted in flashes. He saw a street with heavy traffic. Moving lights. Snow.

Then it was gone. He stared at the house.

"It doesn't make sense."

"Are you getting anything?" she asked.

"Just a street. I'm not sure. I couldn't see enough of it."

She waited quietly, watching the house. Remembering. Her memories crowded into his mind, confusing him.

"Maybe we should drive around a little more," he said. "If we even get near that abandoned house, I might know it."

He couldn't be sure. It didn't always work. He tried to follow what the child might have seen that day, but seeing it through a child's eyes, he could not pick up any clear direction. It was more like a montage, a scattering of scenes.

And fear. He felt himself endlessly moving, and afraid. He saw everything from the height of a small child.

So the boy had wandered away by himself. He had gotten lost and perhaps had been picked up.

"He was in his yard," the mother said. "I couldn't be with him every second. I thought he was safe in the yard."

He turned to look at her. It was the second time she had seemed to latch onto something he was thinking.

Why couldn't he and Libby have that kind of rapport? Instead, there was discord and secrecy. It was the secrecy that bothered him the most. She was blocking something from him. Some part of her life, and it had to do with that job of hers. Perhaps she was trying to earn money so that she could leave him.

Or maybe it was another man. She had been brooding quite a bit and acting defensive. Whatever it was, he would find out somehow. He would catch her with her guard down and see through the wall.

They drove along the Passaic River, but the scenery was all wrong. This was urban, whereas the abandoned house he had seen was isolated somewhere in the country. Someone had picked up the child and driven him—somewhere. He couldn't have walked. There was no place like that within walking distance, especially a small child's walking distance.

He kept thinking of Libby. It shouldn't be like this. He couldn't concentrate when he was bothered by personal things. Maybe he ought to give her a call, if he could find a pay phone.

Suddenly, on a hilly street of tenements and warehouses, he stopped.

He heard Iris catch her breath, probably thinking he had found something.

A grave somewhere. He saw it as though he could see through the earth. He saw clothing and bones. Long bones, and at least three skulls.

He thought they were adults, not young children.

He shook his head. "I'm sorry. I just caught something that might have to do with another case."

"The kidnapping?"

"I don't know. I'm not sure. It just came to me."

"I hope you can find that girl."

"I don't think it was the girl. And it wasn't your son." He started the car.

"Sometimes that happens," he explained. "You're

working on something, and you get all these other things."

"Like a telephone, when you hear other voices," she said.

"Yes, it's like that. Except with a telephone, you can usually tell which are the other voices."

"Is there anything I can do?"

"No. I'm afraid I'm not being very helpful today." He was terribly sorry. She had waited a whole year.

"It's probably a matter of clearing my mind," he went on. "Right now, it's rather cluttered. Maybe we should take a break until tomorrow."

"That's fine," said Iris.

He knew it wasn't fine. She had come this close, and now they had to stop. But he couldn't help it, and she seemed to understand.

He turned the car back toward Fairmont Park. He tried to watch the road, but kept seeing that grave of tumbled bodies. He hated skulls. Death he could accept, but he dealt with the grisliest aspects of it. To him, skulls were a symbol of murder and corruption.

They're mutilated, he realized. Dismembered. That was why they seemed to be packed in such a jumble. And some had been buried for a long time.

He saw hair. Long hair. And red. Again he thought of Libby.

Someone with a fixation for long hair.

"Are you okay?" Iris asked.

He felt dizzy. Sick. It was the vile feeling he got from those images.

"I'm okay." He should not have been driving. "You left your car at the police station?"

"No, I don't have a car. I took a bus."

She directed him to her home. She lived in a sprawling apartment complex, three stories high, although it looked like two, because the first floor was below ground level.

"Could I offer you a cup of coffee?"

She led him to Entrance Number 8 and down a flight of steps to one of the first-floor apartments. He was pleasantly surprised when he entered it. She had furnished it comfortably with an off-white sofa and rug to counteract the sunken location. The dining table, neatly fitted into an alcove, was glass topped, and hanging plants adorned the windows. Off the living room was a single bedroom. A lonely place for a woman who had once had a family.

The kitchen was an L-shaped extension of the living room. Within a few minutes, she brought from it a tray of coffee and cinnamon rolls.

She set it on the coffee table. At one end of the table was a framed snapshot of a baby. Little Ritchie again.

He tried to imagine living through such a tragedy. Would he have blamed his wife, as Richard Knapp had done? Perhaps a momentary lashing out in anguish. But this? She hadn't been careless, any more than the Basiles had been careless. Her husband's cruelty appalled him.

"Have you always been psychic?" she asked.

"I guess so, but it takes a while to realize it. At first, you don't even know what it's all about."

"Did you really see things when you were a child? What sort of things?"

She expected it to be something delightful and childlike.

"Death, mostly," he said. "It has a strong emotional impact. Probably that's why."

"Was it someone close to you?"

He smiled. "The first was our canary. I didn't tell anybody about that. I did tell them when I saw my grandfather's death. I was about six. I assumed they could see it, too, but of course they couldn't. They were furious at me."

"Did he die when you thought he would?"

"To the very night. It rocked them a little, but they said it was because he was old and sick. My guessing the date was just a coincidence."

"It's lucky they didn't think you brought it on by predicting it," she said.

"Yes, that can happen, too. In fact, it did, a couple of years later. We lived in a fourth-floor apartment, and I sensed there was going to be a fire. I told them about it, but they didn't believe me. That night I got out of bed and left the building, and then it started. I was out on the sidewalk when the fire trucks came. My family gave me a hard time about that."

"What sort of hard time?"

"They claimed I must have started it to prove myself right."

"What a nasty thing to say!"

"That was when I began to realize that other people don't necessarily have these flashes of knowing what's coming."

He still remembered the abysmal sense of isolation. He was the "strange" one in the family.

"Did it ever get so they believed you?" she asked.

"I don't know about most of them, but my brother Dalton did. He was several years older. We were still in school when we got invited to go with a bunch of guys on a chartered fishing trip. Both of us were excited. Then I began to get a bad feeling about it. I kept hoping the feeling would go away, but it didn't. Finally I told Dalton. He tried to assure me that everything would be okay. It was a good boat, an experienced skipper, and all that. I wanted to believe him."

Solomon stopped to drink his coffee. She was sitting on the edge of her chair, leaning forward. He hadn't had such an eager audience since he first met Libby six years ago.

And where was Libby now? What had gone wrong?

Damn, he thought, I'm too old for her. That's what it is.

"The day of the trip," he went on, "we got all the way to the pier. I was walking ahead of Dalton, but suddenly I couldn't move. I couldn't make my feet step onto that boat."

"How did you explain it?" she asked. "I mean, to the other people?"

"I told them I didn't feel good. I could tell by the way they looked at me that they thought I was chicken about sailing. I was the youngest there. Dalton took me aside and asked what was really wrong. When I told him, he said he remembered that time of the fire. He backed out of the trip, too, and we went home. In the afternoon, a storm came up. The boat capsized and everybody was drowned. We heard it on the radio that night."

"Oh, how awful," she breathed. Then said, "Dalton must have had a lot to thank you for."

"Well, for a while." He picked up his coffee again. He hoped she wouldn't ask. Dalton had always been his favorite member of the family, and now there was nothing left but his namesake, Solomon's twenty-three-year-old son.

"Did something else happen?"

He realized he had left himself open to the question.

"Something did. It was a nagging feeling that Dalton didn't have much longer to live. I thought the boat accident might have been it, but even afterward, the feeling continued. Then he finished school and went into the army. He never made it back from Korea."

"Oh, Solomon, I'm sorry."

"I am too," he said.

But that had been years ago. Iris's own tragedy was still unfolding.

7

THE sporting goods store was open late that evening, because of a special sale. Libby waited patiently while Neale examined the knives and the guns and fishing gear. To amuse herself, she looked inside the tents that were set up for display.

The largest had two rooms and was furnished with a table, chairs, and cooking gear. On the floor of the smaller room was a double air mattress and two sleeping bags zipped together to make one.

She imagined herself camping with Neale. From the camping trip, a whole new life began to take shape. She saw them taking trips together, living in a modern apartment instead of an old house, and strolling through the mall on Saturdays.

I could do it, she told herself. I could have that, if I really wanted it.

She returned to Neale, who was testing the blade of a knife on his handkerchief. It made a long slit in the fabric.

He ran it across his thumb. A thin streak of blood

appeared and he stared at it, shocked.

"But they're supposed to be sharp," Libby told him. He looked at her blankly, and then back at his hand.

"Poor baby." She took the mutilated handkerchief and wrapped it around his thumb. "What did you think was going to happen?"

"Sharper than I thought," he said.

"Are you going to buy anything?"

"Why, are you getting bored?"

"A little. I'm not turned on by weapons. They don't mean the same thing to women."

"How's that?" he asked, picking up another knife.

"I think to men they're a symbol of virility. Men identify with them. To women, they're just implements."

"Where'd you learn that? From your husband?"

"From observation. I do have a mind of my own."

He smiled and set down the knife. "I'm glad you have a mind of your own. It's a nice mind."

"I wish you'd say it's a good mind."

"Sure it's a good mind. Why so defensive? Does he put you down a lot?"

"All the time, but I don't know if that's the only reason."

"Tell me about it." He guided her toward the door and held it open for her. They continued down the sidewalk, holding hands.

"Tell me about it," he said again. "Tell me about you and your husband."

"Well, actually it's kind of private."

"Of course it is. I don't mean to butt in. It's just

that I want you to be happy, and I don't think you are."

She was touched by his concern. She could not remember when Solomon had ever expressed an interest in her happiness.

"It wasn't always so bad," she said. "For a while we had a really great time together. We were partners, but then—I don't know, it started to change. We weren't together anymore. I was working *for* him, and I didn't feel I had any existence of my own. He could never understand that. He just thought I was being stupid and difficult."

Neale paused briefly to look at a display of dress boots in a men's shoe shop.

"Childish," she went on. "That's his stock rebuttal. I'm much younger than he is, so whenever I disagree with him, I'm childish and selfish. And stupid."

"That's rotten," said Neale.

"He's really a good person."

"Nobody's all bad. Or all good."

"He helps people a lot. He helps—"

"Everybody except you."

It was so true. She was amazed at his insight. Often it seemed as though Solomon's clients saw a better side of him than she did.

She glanced into the window of a children's clothing store. A whole store devoted to babies and small children. She turned away.

"Why stick with it," Neale asked, "if it's not what you want out of life?"

"Because I married him."

She knew what he meant. She knew she ought to go home and never see him again. Solomon would start to worry if she didn't come soon.

But it was only six-thirty. If she went home, she would be expected to prepare dinner, and she had already eaten. Besides, it didn't seem right to end it all so abruptly. At least they could walk back together to where their cars were parked. That would give her time to think.

She walked in silence, trying to get up her courage to tell him it was over, but she couldn't. Not after he had just taken her to dinner. That would be a slap in the face.

When they reached the parking lot, she held his arm and continued past her own car to his. She stood beside him while he unlocked the door. She felt she could do nothing to stop herself. It was as though she were someone else, watching to see what happened next.

They drove for quite a while. Passively she looked out of the window at the city lights.

She did not notice the name of the motel where they stopped, or even the town. In that part of metropolitan New Jersey, just across the river from New York City, one community merged into another with scarcely any interruption.

She waited in the car while Neale took a room. Then he came back to her and drove to one of the units.

It had a double bed. She stared at the bed while he closed and locked the door.

"I never did this before," she said.

"You've never been to a motel?"

"Only to sleep. And never without Solomon."

"You don't have to do anything you don't want to do." He took her in his arms. They still had on their coats. He began to unbutton hers.

After he had taken off her coat, she backed away, suddenly afraid of surrendering everything. She took off her shoes and her knee-high stockings and then stopped.

"I can't," she said. "I just never did this before."

"That's all right." She thought he seemed relieved, and it surprised her.

They slipped off the rest of their clothes and lay in bed, but did not make love.

"I'm sorry," she whispered.

"No, really, this is fine." He held her and kissed her. "Maybe next time."

Next time. He hadn't given up on her.

"I really do like you," she told him. "I just can't—"

"I understand."

Her mind raced on. Maybe, with Neale, she could manage to get pregnant. Sometimes it was a combination, and not just one person's fault. She could have her child, and Solomon would never know.

Or perhaps, being Solomon, he would.

Neale murmured, "I like you so much."

He hadn't said he loved her. Maybe that would come later.

"I like you, too. So much." She felt guilty for saying it. It seemed even worse than getting into bed with him. If God didn't punish her, she would probably do something to punish herself.

And then she thought sorrowfully, *Don't I have a right to anything?*

How could she be so unlucky? At last, here was a man who treated her as an equal. Who listened to her and respected her opinions and ideas. For the first time in her life she felt like a worthwhile person, and yet the circumstances were all wrong.

"Do you think this is wrong?" she asked.

"I don't know if it's wrong. All I know is, you're getting to be very important to me."

Important to him. It was exactly what she needed.

He pushed her flat on the bed and covered her body with his. He kissed her shoulders, stroked her neck with his thumb. He groaned and leaned forward to kiss her Adam's apple.

She fought against the weight on her throat. Frantically she pushed him away, crying aloud and struggling to breathe. Then she sat still, disheveled and gasping.

"What happened?" he asked.

"I couldn't breathe. I'm sorry."

"Why are you sorry?"

"For acting like that. Getting so scared. I really thought I couldn't breathe."

"Guess I got a little carried away," he said.

"It's really all right. I just panicked."

"Are you okay now?"

"Oh, yes, I'm fine. Really."

He pulled her toward him and she rested against his chest. He did care. He cared about her.

"I don't know what to do," she said.

"Just take it easy."

"I mean about Solomon. I think I love him, in a way, but I don't want to stay with him. It's too hard on me."

"Then don't."

"I can't help it. I feel pulled in half, thinking of him, thinking of myself."

"It's significant that you put him first," Neale said. "I think that's what's stopping you."

"I can't help that, either. Look, I never talked about this to anybody, so don't repeat it, will you?"

"Who would I repeat it to?" he asked with a smile.

"Anybody."

She longed to tell him her death fantasy, the plane crash or the heart attack, but she couldn't. It would make her sound too brutal, and she wasn't. Perhaps that was her trouble.

It was after nine when they left the motel. No longer evening, but nighttime. What would she tell Solomon?

It was a sparkling night, chilly, but with a hint of spring softness in the air. Neale drove her back to the parking lot where she had left her car.

On the way home she tried to compose herself, to get him out of her mind. To get the things they had talked about out of her mind. She called back the stone wall. A high, impenetrable wall.

Solomon would see it in his own mind. He would know what it was for—to hide her thoughts from him. Of course he would wonder about the thoughts that needed so much protection. He would try to break down her wall, and he might succeed. His mind was stronger than hers.

As she approached the house, she was surprised to see it dark. She felt a moment of panic, wondering if they were supposed to have gone somewhere and she had forgotten. Then she saw his car in the driveway.

Something must have happened. She parked her own car quickly and got out. Maybe this was it. Maybe he had had a stroke or a heart attack.

She fumbled at the lock, dropping her keys. Finally she was inside. She switched on a light.

"Solomon?"

Through the darkened dining room she saw a glow in the kitchen. Then the refrigerator door thudded closed and the light disappeared.

Solomon's voice said, "Have your fun while you can, Libby. You won't be young forever."

She saw his outline in the doorway, and the gleam of a water glass in his hand. Bottled water. It was almost all he drank.

"I didn't know you were home, Solomon. I had to work late. They were awfully busy. And then one of the people at the office—we went out and had coffee, and—I should have called."

The outline moved closer.

"Yes," he said quietly, "you should have."

He knows, she thought. If he wanted to know, he would. There was nothing she could hide from him.

Nothing.

Ever.

8

"Don't you think you're being rather childish?" Solomon asked.

She thought of going to the office, even though it was Saturday. But they didn't expect her and they wouldn't want her. They had another receptionist for weekends.

"You keep telling me I never sit down and talk to you," he went on. "Now I'm willing to talk, and you're sulking."

"I am not."

She sat at the breakfast table in her blue housecoat and stirred her coffee. Solomon was already dressed. At least he would be out for a while, doing his broadcast.

He was watching her. She could feel it. She tried to conjure up her stone wall. He must have seen it and known its purpose. She had to concentrate.

She embellished the wall. Part of it was covered with soft green moss. Velvet moss, and ferns. It was not a flat wall, not completely perpendicular. It had uneven tiers and protruding stones. A waterfall trickled down the moss.

There was a wall like it in the shopping mall, but she did not want her own creation in such a public place. It became a natural rock formation deep in a forest, and she was the only one there. At its base was a moss-lined pool. She took off her shoes and waded.

The water tumbled on down the side of a mountain. From time to time Neale would appear below her, barefooted, with his pants rolled to his knees. He was climbing toward her. She had to keep banishing him.

Solomon began to laugh. "Don't you realize how absurd this is?"

"I don't think so. I think it's beautiful."

"Absurd," he said again. "A man with five o'clock shadow."

"What man?"

She hadn't realized that, in her imagined scene, Neale was unshaven. He had very dark hair, and a growth of beard would tint his face late in the day. It had done that yesterday. But in the glimpses she caught of him now, his expression was gentle and sweet.

"Taking an outside job really paid off, didn't it?" said Solomon.

"Yes, it did," she answered. "I have more respect for myself now."

"And more men."

"Well—of course there are men. After all, you have female clients. That's just the way the world is set up."

She could play at his game of deflecting an argument. All it took was a certain amount of aggressiveness.

"You and I were working together," he reminded her. "Building our life together. I thought that was what you wanted."

"It didn't seem like together. It seemed as if you were the boss and I was the secretary."

"I may get a little impatient at times—"

"That," she said, "is only part of the problem."

"Then I guess I just don't understand the problem." He turned and left the room.

Solomon was sorry he had been so abrupt. He didn't know how to handle these scenes. What could he say to her?

Why, he wondered angrily, did she have to be so unreasonable?

An unpleasant idea nagged at him. She might be unreasonable, but maybe that wasn't all of it. Maybe he was avoiding something.

He couldn't think about that now. He had a busy day ahead of him. There was the radio show at ten, and then an hour of meditation to clear his mind. He was scheduled to meet Iris Knapp at one o'clock. And over all, he had to search for Amy Basile's body and her kidnapper.

Libby did not accompany him to the studio, as she used to do. Nor was she around afterward when he closed himself in his study to meditate. He knew she was home, because her car was there, but she had apparently, and wisely, decided to keep her distance. That way, they wouldn't rub each other raw.

He sat down at his desk and closed his eyes, but his mind would not clear. He kept seeing a smiling man with five o'clock shadow, climbing the rocks beside a waterfall.

He did not understand why that image was so clear, when the others were not. It must have been a memory of something very important to her. Someone she had dredged out of the past as a balm for her present dissatisfaction. He wondered if she was still in touch with the man, or knew where to find him.

He tried to shake off the image. It was not relevant to his work. He must not let her and her petty moods interfere.

The meditation was not a success that day. He gave it up and reached for the envelope Iris Knapp had given him.

He studied the photograph, looking into the clear gray eyes, questioning them. He saw a group of letters. *C-A-N* or *M*. A road name?

He began to grow excited. He opened a map of Passaic County and spread it face down on the desk. He held his hand over it until he began to feel the place. He should have done this sooner. He lowered his hand with the index finger pointed and grooved the spot where it had touched. Then he turned over the map.

The spot he had picked was not far from Camp Road, in an open place near a lake, where no other roads were shown. There must have been a way in. He saw a large white boulder under a tree. He knew it was an unmarked intersection. There would be no road sign. Only the stone.

He put on his coat and left the house. As he left, he

was aware of Libby watching him from an upstairs window. He felt something strange. A kind of yearning.

He felt it was for him, but it couldn't have been. She was too engrossed in her childish daydreams. What did she think life was all about, anyway?

When he reached Iris's apartment, he was surprised to find her wearing the green pantsuit.

"I thought it might help," she said. "I thought maybe you could get something from it."

"I may have something already," he told her, thinking that she looked very nice and very vulnerable that day.

"What do you mean?"

"I found a place on the map. It's worth checking out, anyway."

She got into his car and they drove toward Camp Road.

"I don't understand," she said. "You told me how it works, but I don't understand how you'd know."

"I don't understand how I know, either," Solomon replied. "It's something I see in my mind. It's like a television screen. But it isn't always visual. Sometimes I hear the answer. Sometimes I just seem to know it."

"What did you see this time?"

"I found an approximate place on the map. And what I saw was a big white stone at the side of the road."

"That's not what you saw before."

"No. I think it might lead us to it, though."

"I see." She was silent for a while, and then said, "He's dead, isn't he?"

"I'm afraid he probably is."

She nodded. "I just want to know. It's a terrible thing, to keep hoping. It takes it all out of you. I just want to get on with my life."

He reflected that she was young enough to do that. Find another man, have another child. She could never replace the first child. The loss would always be there, but she could still have a life.

He thought again of Libby. She, too, kept saying she wanted to have a life. He must remember to tell her that happiness comes from inside. If she was a basically dissatisfied person, no superficial changes were going to make any difference.

They were driving north on Camp Road. Through the trees, he could see houses. The place was not as remote as it appeared to be.

He knew where he was supposed to turn off. That road had been on the map. And then he would watch for the white boulder.

He asked, "What was he wearing?"

She lowered her hands from her face.

"Your son," he said. "What was he wearing the day he disappeared?"

"A blue snowsuit."

"I'm sorry to bring it all back to you. Light or dark?"

"Medium. Sort of royal blue. It was bright. Who could—how could he get this far? And why?"

"That's for the police to find out. I think we're almost there."

He slowed the car and put on his turn signal. He began to have a feeling of rightness, as though he were being guided by an invisible beam.

The road led up a hill and through a stand of pine trees. Beyond it was a yellow house with a tennis court.

Slowly now. The trees, the countryside, were beginning to look like what he had seen. There were low hills and woods. On his left was a red barn with a sign that said "Antiques." On his right, a wooded area. In summer, he knew, it would be dark with trees. Up ahead was a break in the trees that might be a road.

And there was the boulder.

A narrow road, its tarred surface in wretched condition, led off to the right, past the boulder. He took it. Even at twenty miles an hour, his car bumped into the potholes. He hoped it wouldn't be far.

The woods thinned. There were fields with tall meadow grasses, bare and bleak in the early March wind. They were getting close. The terrain was exactly right. Fields and wind. A tall tree.

He saw the elm from the top of a small hill, as they rounded a bend. Even with its leaves off, he knew it was an elm by its shape. He began to feel a strange excitement, a fluttering in his chest. An overgrown hedge bordered the property. The two stone posts...

"That's *it!*" cried Iris. "That's exactly what you said."

She turned to look at him, and for an instant he caught the look of incredulity, almost horror, that he had seen so often. He had seen it when his grandfather died, and after his family had been rescued from the fire. As though he had somehow caused it, or been in league with the devil.

"Yes, there it is," he said and stopped the car. A

rusted chain was strung between the two posts. He got out of the car and went to examine it. Both ends were attached to eyelets embedded in the posts. There were two parts to the chain, and where they met in the middle, they were fastened with a padlock. A new one. He made a mental note of that.

"We'll have to walk in," he said.

She got out of the car. Her face was drawn and her eyes distant. He lifted the chain to let her under and then went under it himself. They started up the driveway. It went around a bend, and then they saw the house.

"It's so lonely here," she said plaintively.

"Just remember," he told her, "Ritchie's probably gone. If we find anything, it won't be Ritchie."

"Yes."

He took her arm to give her comfort. He thought of his own two children, grown up and working. All in all, in spite of losing his brother and having marital troubles, his life had been a pretty good one. Helping people like Iris was his way of paying for its goodness.

She patted his hand. "I'm glad you're here." He thought it ironic that he seemed to get along with everybody except his wife.

They stood looking at the house. At the tawny stucco that matched the dried meadow grasses. The boarded windows, the leathery-leaved rhododendrons.

"What do we do now?" she asked. He hadn't told her about his vision, seeing the child's face as though in water. On the map, there had been a lake, but his vision of the house had been clear. It might be a well or a cistern. Whatever it was, he wanted to find it first. He led her to the front steps.

"Why don't you wait here?" he told her. "Or would you rather go back to the car? It might be warmer."

"No, I'll stay here." She sat down on the top step and prepared to wait.

As he started around the house, he looked back at her, sitting and waiting for him to find her dead child. Again he felt that he had been fortunate. Even though it was his lot to share her pain and feel the child's death, it was still secondhand. If he could separate himself from that, his own life was tranquil by comparison.

In back of the house was an overgrown, terraced garden. Dead flowers and weeds stood blackened by frost and snow. The meadow had encroached here, too, leaving its plumy grasses on the tiers of rock and earth. He looked about for a well or a garden pool.

In a hollow at the foot of the garden, just where the hill began to rise, he noticed a clump of rushes. Water plants. He heard a pheasant screech. It flapped away as he approached.

Hidden by the waving rushes was a small, shallow pond. A crust of ice still bordered its shore. He stood among the waist-high stalks and looked out into the water where, down among the mud and roots, was a glimmer of bright blue.

9

*H*E climbed back up to the house and around to the front, where she waited. She stood up when she saw him coming. He held her hands while he tried to think of a way to say it.

"Where?" she asked.

"There's a little pond down in back. Don't go and look. You can't see much anyway." He started to lead her toward the car.

She held back. "Where are we going?"

"To call the police."

She seemed bewildered. She hadn't thought beyond this moment.

"I guess so," she said finally. And then, "If you couldn't see much, are you sure?"

"I'm sure."

He had been right, of course. Hours later he took Iris back to her apartment and then drove home. He had hated to leave her, but there was nothing more he could do. She had telephoned some of her relatives, and her parents were on their way from Perth Amboy.

When he reached home, he saw that Libby was there. The lights were on and her car was in the driveway. He parked behind it and turned off the engine. Before he could leave the car, his mind opened for a moment like the shutter of a camera, showing him a strange, scattered scene.

He blinked. The picture was gone. He tried to recall it.

Pieces of things, scattered about. He realized that it was a pencil drawing. Pieces of people. Arms and legs. A head.

"Damn," he muttered as he slammed the car door. He was sick of all this horror.

He caught a glimpse of the Basile house. His vision had had something to do with the kidnapping. He remembered the grave he had seen. He remembered that he had thought it contained dismembered bodies. That part of it made sense, but why a penciled drawing?

He entered the house and found Libby alone in the living room, watching television.

"Where were you?" she asked.

"Finding a kid. Been missing a year."

"And you found her?"

"Him. Dead."

As he looked at her, he saw the drawings again. *Not Libby. Not her!*

He had given himself away. She asked, "What's the matter?"

He remembered the hair, long hair, that seemed to arouse the man. Amy Basile had long hair, sleek and glossy, almost black. Libby's, falling to well below her shoulders, was a stunning mahogany color.

He could feel his face drawing into a look of pain. He said, "I wish you'd cut it."

"What?" She reached back and smoothed her hair.

"I told you, he has a thing about hair. The kidnapper."

"Nobody's going to kidnap me," she said. "What would he get out of it?"

"I also told you it's not the money. It's the girls he wants."

"I'm hardly a girl." She glared at him, thinking he was belittling her again.

"I only want to keep you safe."

"I can keep myself safe. In the first place, I never hitchhike."

"Amy Basile was taken out of her home."

She flounced impatiently. "Solomon, she's a child. I know a few things."

"I hope so."

That was wrong. He should have said he trusted her, but he was worried. He went upstairs to change out of his hiking boots. When he sat down on the bed to untie them, something bright caught his eye. It was on the floor, halfway under the edge of the bedspread. He picked it up.

A gold pen, certainly not his. He didn't think she owned one, either. It looked expensive, but he did not have time to study it before a mass of impressions crowded in.

He went back downstairs. She waved him to be quiet. Her show was just ending. When the commercial came on, she was ready to listen.

He turned down the sound on the television. "Where did this come from?"

She made no attempt to take it, but studied it as he held it out to her.

"Where did you find it?" she asked.

"Under the bed."

She shrugged.

He said, "It's not mine. Did you go out and buy something like this?"

At last he had her attention, but it was angry attention.

"There you go again, acting as if I can't spend a cent without your permission, even when I earn the money myself."

"That's not why I asked. I get a funny feeling about this pen. I see a room, like a bedroom, all white, with a white wicker desk. I see an open window."

"So?"

"It came from that room."

"Probably. I borrowed it from somebody at the office and forgot to return it. I don't know what their room looks like."

"It's somebody who seems to be a respectable person."

"She is," said Libby.

"It's a man," he told her, unable to conceal his triumph. "But the room that I see is hardly a man's room."

"Well, Solomon, I can't help that."

"It seems to me," he went on, "that he came through the window and left it open."

"Who did?"

"The person I'm talking about. He's someone people think well of. They like him. That's how he comes across."

"And?"

He dropped the pen onto her lap.

"I can see a lot of things. I see shoplifting. Burglary. I see guns. This man gets a thrill from climbing in windows and breaking into homes. He steals things, but that's only secondary. It's the breaking in that counts."

"Oh, baloney!" she cried.

"He wears a mask," Solomon went on. "A mask of sanity, but inside—" He drew a long breath. "Inside is something so deep and terrible that I don't know how to describe it."

She kept a calm face, but he saw that he had shaken her.

"Deep and terrible by whose standards?" she asked.

"By human standards. The man is dangerous. He's sick."

"Then it's not his fault." She was speaking abstractly. She no longer related their conversation to the person who had given her the pen.

"It's not the man's fault that he's sick," Solomon agreed, "but it's his fault that he won't recognize the problem and try to help himself. Maybe that's part of his pathology."

She dropped the theoretical stance and again became defensive.

"You don't know what you're talking about."

10

*H*E wished he had kept the pen. He might have learned more about the man who gave it to her. The whole thing was important. Either she didn't understand its importance, or she preferred to deny it.

He stayed at his desk until almost midnight. He even considered sleeping in his study, because he knew she had lied to him, but he couldn't prove it. That made him angry.

He was about to go upstairs and get a blanket, when the telephone rang. He tried to reach for it. His hand stopped in midair. In his mind he saw a large red *B* and caught the image of a gas tank.

After that, he could move again. He picked up the phone.

Mike Tarasco said, "Sorry if I woke you, Sol."

"You didn't," Solomon answered. "What are you doing? You're not on duty, are you?"

"I thought you'd want to know. They arrested a guy in Atlantic City." Mike sounded jubilant.

"What for?"

"At one of the casinos. He had a roll of the ransom

money on him. They figure he was trying to launder it."

"Who was it, do you know?"

"He wouldn't give his name," Mike replied. "Says he found the money in his car. You ever heard such bullshit? I'm leaving in a while to go down there and pick him up. I wouldn't miss it for a million bucks."

"Just when you rang, I saw something. A red *B* and a gas tank."

"Oh, hell. Bobby Redfield."

"Who's that?" asked Solomon.

"A punk. He's a regular here. If it's him, he might as well have given his name. We've got a dossier, pictures, fingerprints, the works. He's a druggie. I wouldn't have figured him for the kidnapper. That takes a certain amount of brains."

"Don't take my word for it."

"Who else could it be? He even lives over on the south side, near the gas tank. Well, we'll see when he gets here."

"Thanks for letting me know, Mike."

Solomon hung up the phone and sat thinking. Something about all this didn't sit right. He tried to figure out what it was. Maybe he felt uneasy because of the thing about Libby. He wished she would realize that she was driving him crazy and hampering his work.

But she wouldn't realize it. She was stubborn and selfish. He went upstairs to the linen closet, found a spare blanket, and lay down on the couch in his study.

* * *

By morning, newspaper headlines announced a "break in the kidnapping." A sullen Bobby Redfield had been transported back to Fairmont Park from his luxurious hotel in Atlantic City.

Bobby was twenty-five years old, the product of a troubled, disadvantaged black family. He had been brushing with the law for most of his life, and had served time—petty time for petty crimes.

Never before had he done anything like the kidnapping. The detectives who had worked around the clock that day and night still found it difficult to reconcile a previously uncrackable case with Bobby's bumbling, drug-rotted mind. Even less comprehensible was his elaborate scheme for exchanging the ransom money.

"I don't get it," Mike Tarasco kept saying. "I just don't get it."

"That don't mean he didn't do it," replied Al Mounsey, who had gone with Mike to bring Bobby back. "They caught him with his pants down, so to speak. He was acting suspicious, and that don't sound too smart, either."

"They probably got suspicious of a jerk like Redfield having all that money," Mike speculated. "He's strictly small time. His *brain* is small time. I don't know how he did it."

"Might be another brain in there somewhere," said Mounsey.

By the time the questioning started, Bobby was ready to talk. He seemed quite pleased with having thought up the kidnap scheme and declined to share the credit with anyone else.

"Yeah, I took her," he said. "I gassed her."

"With what?"

"Chloroform."

"Who helped you, Bobby?"

He stared at them with sullen, clouded eyes. His fix was wearing off, and he was starting to get irritable.

"Nobody! You think I'm gonna split that with anybody?"

"Where'd you get the chloroform?"

"Same place I—" He clammed up. They didn't pursue it, but asked what had happened when he gassed the girl.

"She went limp," Bobby said. "Like she passed out. I carried her outside and put her in my car. I put a blanket on her. When I got home, I looked under the blanket and she was dead. It was an accident."

"Yeah?"

"Yeah. I didn't know how much gas to use. She was trying to fight me. I musta kept it on too long. Shit, man, I didn't mean to kill her. I wanted the money."

"Then what did you do?"

"I got scared. I dumped her."

"Where?"

"Near a road somewheres. I don't know, it was dark."

The questioning went on. Bobby knew details of the kidnapping that had not been released to the public. By the time he had gone to pieces and was slipped a pacifying fix, they knew they had their man. They also had $4,000 of the ransom money. He said he could not remember what he had done with the rest of it.

Bobby was arraigned on charges of first-degree kidnapping and first-degree grand larceny. They had only his word that the girl was dead, but they didn't really need an additional homicide charge. Kidnapping was enough.

The next morning, Libby expected to hear from Neale again. They hadn't seen each other all weekend, but it was almost lunchtime before he called. Her heart gave a lurch when she heard his voice. She thought maybe she had put him off by holding back in the motel on Friday night. She had thought he understood, but maybe he didn't.

And now he was calling. She had only an instant of happiness before his next words plunged her back into depression.

"I don't think I'll be able to see you today." He sounded regretful, but that didn't mean he was.

"What happened?" she asked.

"It's work. I've been busy since yesterday with a new client."

She wondered why it couldn't wait, considering how slowly the court system worked, but she really knew nothing about law.

"It's going to keep me tied up for a while," he went on.

"Well, I hope you make a lot of money," she told him lightly.

"I'm not making any money. Sometimes I do that, if it's a big case and the person's broke. You can learn a lot."

"A big case?" Solomon had told her about Mike's call. Solomon was not one to maintain a stony silence, even though he had slept in the study last night. She assumed he told her mainly because the news was too exciting to keep to himself.

"I can't say anything," Neale explained, "but I think you guessed it."

"And you're taking it for free?" She wondered about the ransom money. Basile had paid half the ransom, and there must have been a lot still floating around, considering they had only found four thousand on Bobby Redfield in Atlantic city. Why couldn't Bobby come up with a lawyer's fee?

"I told you, I do that sometimes. And it's a big case. It'll be worth my while."

"Well, I think that's nice of you." She spoke hesitantly. Was it really nice to defend the kidnapper and killer of a young girl?

Neale laughed. "You don't sound too convinced. Well, the way I see it, we all help each other. That's what people are supposed to do."

"But if he's guilty, don't try to get him off. That's horrible, what he did."

"What he's charged with," Neale corrected her. "We'll see what happens. I shouldn't even be talking about it, so keep it to yourself, okay?"

Neale looked forward to the case. He had never handled a major court case before, and this was a big one. He had already decided on his point of attack.

The jail seemed a hell of a public place to be conferring with his client. He insisted that they keep their voices down.

"What for?" Bobby asked dolefully. "They already convicted me."

"That was not a conviction, Bobby, it was an arraignment. You know that. Now get a grip on yourself. These are pretty serious charges, and you already confessed, so here's what we're going to do. We're going to go for an insanity plea."

"Hey, man, I ain't crazy!"

"It's your best defense. They'll put you in a hospital instead of a prison. You could rot in prison. This is the smart way to do it, but it's going to take planning. You know you'll have to talk to some doctors. If they don't think you're disturbed, you go to the slammer."

"You mean I gotta act crazy."

"Don't you dare act crazy. They can see through that. You don't have to act anything. You *have* got problems, Bobby."

The young man's lips drew back in a sneer. "What are you talking about?"

"I know your record," Neale said. "I know all about those break-ins. You weren't just after money, were you? People who break into houses, Bobby, that's a sign of sexual disturbance."

"I ain't got no sexual disturbance! I can make it every time."

"No, you can't. You're on drugs."

"You know," Bobby clenched his hands menacingly, "you keep talking to me like that, and—"

"Not in jail, you won't," said Neale. "There are guards all over the place."

"I can fire you," Bobby taunted.

"Not really. You didn't hire me. I'm doing this for free. I'm trying to help you, and you'd better listen, because I know the best way to help you. If you get sent to a hospital, maybe they can get you over these problems."

"What problems?"

"Getting your kicks from breaking and entering."

Bobby sat hunched, staring at the floor. He looked defeated. He had no bargaining power and couldn't even indulge in his usual swift physical reprisals.

"That kind of thing," Neale went on, "is symptomatic of a sexual perversion. The shrinks know that and the judges know it. They know it's a compulsion. They know you can't help it, any more than you can help, say, the hiccups."

"They gonna send me to a nut farm?"

"It's better than a prison. You'll get help. What did prison ever do for you?"

Bobby shrugged.

"Okay, then." Neale moved closer to him and dropped his voice still lower.

"First you tell me everything you can about the kidnapping. Tell me how you thought of it, how you led up to it. You started with the girl, right? You saw her leaving the house once on her bicycle. You saw the way she looked at you when you sat in your car, watching her. You saw all that long hair streaming out in the wind...."

11

MIKE Tarasco replayed the tape of Bobby's confession, listening to how he had watched the girl, stalked her, and finally seen his chance when her parents went out for the evening.

"How did you know they were going out for the evening?" one of the interrogators asked.

"Uh, because, uh, they wuz all dressed up."

Pretty dumb, Mike thought, but spontaneous. It was good, the way the case was shaping up.

He played the tape again.

"Damn," he said aloud, "that's three different places where he thinks he might have dumped her. And they're all vague."

"*He's* vague," replied Farley O'Brien at the next desk. "He burnt himself out with them drugs. We're on our own, Mike."

"I know it." Mike reached for the telephone. If he didn't do this of his own accord, the Basiles would insist on it anyway. He called Solomon Thayer.

"Whenever you get a chance," he said, "I'll have a transcription for you, okay? That was pretty good, what you did with the Knapp kid."

Solomon muttered noncommittally. Mike knew he hated finding bodies. He hated telling the parents, although, for many, it was a relief to have it over.

"You were right about the kidnapping," he added. "It wasn't just the money. A lot of it was kicks. Too bad, a kid like that. She should have been safe in her own home."

In the afternoon, when he had finished with his clients, Solomon went to the police station and looked over the transcript of Bobby's statement.

"It isn't right," he said.

"What do you mean, it isn't right?" asked Mike.

"That stuff about the car. She was in the trunk, and there wasn't any blanket."

Mike leaned back in his swivel chair.

"If I may say so, Redfield was on the scene."

"It isn't right," Solomon repeated.

"He was pretty zonked on drugs. Might have made a mistake. He couldn't even remember what he did with the body."

"He was just guessing."

"Looks that way."

"It isn't a matter of not remembering," said Solomon. "He never knew. He's not the kidnapper."

"Hey, wait a minute. The guy confessed."

"That's unusual?"

"No, but he knew a lot of stuff he wouldn't know unless he did it."

Solomon was adamant. "Some of the stuff he knows isn't right. Like how he transported the body and where he dumped it. She's underground someplace, in a shaft or vault. Some kind of underground structure. If he were the one who put her there, he ought to know."

"Forgive me, Sol, but are you ever wrong?"

"Of course I am, a lot of times."

"Well, then..."

"But I don't think I'm wrong about this."

"Why not?"

"It's clear. I can feel and see it clearly."

"And that proves it's right?"

"Mike, we've known each other for years. You know I sometimes see things but interpret them wrong. Other times, yes, I do get faulty perceptions. I can't explain this, but—"

"But what?"

"I don't know."

Mike could see that his friend was shaken. He thought something might be bothering Sol, but he didn't ask about it. They knew each other well enough so Sol would tell him if he wanted to.

"Do you feel like going with us," he asked, "to check out some of these places?"

"I guess I could," said Solomon, "but I don't know if I'll be any help."

They set out immediately, accompanied by Farley O'Brien. Only a few hours remained before dark. Mike had jotted down notes from the transcript, all the information Redfield had given as to possible dumping sites, but it wasn't enough.

"Beside a road," Mike said in disgust. "That's a big help. What else has New Jersey got besides roads?"

"It figures to be somewhere around Fairmont Park," Farley offered.

"Yeah, thanks."

"The woods," said Solomon. "Doesn't he mention some woods?"

"That's like saying find some sand in the Sahara."

"There's a woods—" Solomon began, and pressed his hand to his forehead.

"Yeah?"

"A chain link fence with a gate. And the color yellow."

"What are you talking about?"

"A big gate. Cars can drive through it."

"An army post?" asked Farley.

"Nothing like that around here," said Mike.

"Some kind of security area," Farley began.

"Near a woods," said Solomon.

Mike studied his notes. "He said it was on a hill."

"It is." Solomon felt that he was looking up at the gate.

Yellow. The yellow was on the gate. A rectangle. Maybe a sign.

"Is there anything like that around here," he asked, "with a gate like that, that has a yellow sign on it?"

"The landfill!" exclaimed Farley. "He dumped her in the landfill!"

Mike said, "That's crazy. That's no place to hide a body."

"Why not?"

"People go in there all the time. You can't hide something."

"You can," Farley maintained, "if you put it under stuff."

"I wouldn't hide anything there unless I wanted it found," muttered Mike. Farley took it as an assent, turned the car around, and headed toward the landfill just outside the city limit.

As soon as they started up the hill, Mike asked, "Does it look right?"

"Yes." Solomon was ashamed that he hadn't recognized the vision. "Except, when I see it, the gate's closed."

"It's open now," said Farley. "There's your yellow sign. It says open eight to four, Monday through Saturday."

They drove through the gate and parked next to the glass recycling bins. Mike started to open his door.

"She's not in here," said Solomon.

Mike paused with one foot out of the car. "What do you mean, she's not in here?"

"She can't be. When I see it, the gate is closed."

"You said that already."

"Don't you see? It was closed when he came here. There's no other way in."

"Well, okay. So it's another big gate. It sounds like a plant entrance to me."

"No, it's this. It looks exactly like this, but after hours. Wasn't there something about woods?" Solomon pointed toward the left. A densely wooded area spilled down over the hillside.

Mike stared dully at the woods as he pulled in his foot and closed the door. "We gotta dig through all that?"

"Smells better than the dump, anyway," Farley

observed. They drove back out through the gate and parked at the edge of the road.

"Sol, you lead the way," said Mike.

Solomon stood resting against the car, his hands in his pockets. All he could see was a man looking up a waterfall. It had nothing to do with the job at hand. He couldn't get his mind off Libby and the idea that she must be seeing another man. Distantly he heard Mike speaking to him.

"I'm trying to concentrate," Solomon replied.

Mike said, "Oh—sorry," and the two detectives went into the woods. Farley carried a small shovel. If they found anything, they would send for reinforcements.

A cold breeze blew, ruffling Solomon's hair. He tried to pull himself together, to forget Libby for the time being and leave his mind clear to receive impressions. The breeze made his eyes water. He felt the cold seeping through his sheepskin jacket.

That was impossible. The jacket was impenetrable. The cold must be somewhere else.

Underground. There was no wind, only a horrible, inescapable, pervasive cold.

She'll die, he thought.

He shook his head. That was silly. She couldn't possibly be alive, buried underground like that. He tried to see her again, but the image would not return. The breeze subsided and he felt a faint warmth on his face and hands from the late winter sun.

He did not know how long he waited before he saw them coming. They were walking rapidly. Farley waved the shovel. Solomon looked up at the sky and saw that the sun had moved. It must have been quite a while.

"There's something there," Mike said, opening the car door and picking up the microphone. He asked for more men, more shovels. A backhoe.

"It's going to be dark soon," said Farley.

"We'll get in an hour's digging," Mike replied. "How are you doing, Sol?"

"Nothing. What did you find?"

"Plastic. Just a little piece sticking out of the ground. One of those silver garbage bags. It's a body, all right, but—"

"Yes?"

"Not hers. It can't be. It's been there too long."

"Female?"

"Can't tell. It's—We can't tell much of anything, except that now we've got another homicide."

"How do you know it's homicide?"

"We don't," said Mike. "I should have called it a probable homicide. The thing is, you see, it's all in pieces."

12

*T*HEY stood at the site where the body had been unearthed.

"Got any ideas?" asked Mike.

Solomon stared at the empty hole. He felt something hard and unyielding pressing around him. Cold, like frozen ground.

"About what?" he asked.

Mike nodded toward the pit. "We need an identity."

Solomon started to shake his head. It turned into a shudder.

"There are more," he said.

"Yeah? Where?"

Four policemen with spades were probing the ground in an ever-widening circle. The backhoe had dug all around the tree under which the body had been found. So far, they had discovered nothing further.

"Another grave." Solomon turned away, feeling something tighten around his throat. "I don't know where."

"What's wrong?"

"They were strangled."

"Can you see it?"

"Feel it." Solomon's voice was strained. He heard the scraping of a shovel next to his ear. He looked up. Two policemen were digging far away. He felt dried leaves against his face. He knew that a girl had lain nearly dead, unable to move, hearing the murderer dig her grave.

"God!" he cried, as he bolted toward the car. It had to end. He didn't want to know the rest.

Mike ran after him. "It's rough, huh?"

Still gasping for air, Solomon gave a bitter laugh at the understatement. Mike stared at him, shocked and sorry. Another car drove up. A policeman got out, leading a German shepherd dog. Solomon watched them go into the woods.

"I hope that dog does better than I can," he said.

"You're doing okay," Mike told him. It wasn't true, and they both knew it.

"I know there's another body. I'll try again. I'm sorry. It was horrible." Solomon started back toward the woods. He wished he had brought his own car. He wanted nothing more than to leave this scene and go home.

They returned to the excavation made by the backhoe.

"I know there's another grave," he repeated. "There are two. Two together."

"Graves?" asked Mike.

"Bodies. They're buried together, one on top of the other."

"Okay, Sol, just take it easy. You think it's here, in this woods?"

Solomon looked around. It was not even a very big woods. It extended over the side of the hill, and then stopped at the edge of a new apartment complex. He began to walk. A policeman, searching the ground for any sign of disturbance, looked up at him. Solomon felt the man's doubt. He felt that they were laughing at him. Only Mike believed in him. He had felt doubt before, but it never mattered. He knew what he could do.

Now he wasn't sure. He had not felt this way since he was a child, first beginning to discover his gifts. He kept thinking of Libby. Why must he think of Libby? He saw the man at the waterfall.

A much younger man. Years younger than he. She hadn't admitted it, but she didn't have to. All this time he had thought they had a good thing going. He should have guessed this might happen. It must be a strain, living with someone who could read what you were thinking. He should have understood.

Something screamed in his mind, *That's not it at all.*

He ignored the scream. That had to be it. That, and his age. He'd have to be a lot dumber than he was not to figure it out.

"Hey!" called Mike's voice. "Where ya going?"

Solomon turned around. Through the trees, he could see Mike at the top of the hill. He hadn't realized that he had walked so far.

Mike cupped his hands and called again. "You got something?"

He had to find something. It was around here somewhere, but he couldn't find it. He remembered the policeman's skeptical look. It had been like that when he was a child and they didn't believe him. He had been so lonely then.

He climbed back up the hill.

"Maybe it's not here," he said to Mike. "I thought it was here."

Mike glanced at his watch. "It's getting late. The sun's going down."

Libby would be coming home. Maybe.

"Got any more ideas?" Mike asked. "Any identification?"

"Nothing."

"Something on your mind, huh?"

"You guessed it."

Mike's hand landed heavily on his back. "Take it easy. Maybe Bobby'll tell us himself."

"He can't tell you anything."

"You still think he didn't do it, huh?"

"I know he didn't."

"Look, Sol, the man confessed."

Solomon neither looked nor listened. He raised his head. This was a new feeling, and it had nothing to do with the afternoon's events. From somewhere, he could smell danger.

"Mike, can you spare somebody to drive me back to my car? I've got to get home."

"What's wrong?"

"It's Libby."

"In trouble?"

"I don't know."

"I'll take you myself." Mike called to a nearby officer, "Tell O'Brien I'll be back in a couple of minutes."

It was well after five. Getting toward six o'clock. Libby still waited for a phone call, but knew it was hopeless. He had said he would be busy. She knew what that meant. He didn't want to see her anymore.

She couldn't really blame him, after the way she had acted. He would find an unmarried girl who didn't have so many scruples. She had had her chance at a wonderful man and lost him.

The office was closing. She would have to leave, because she didn't have a key for locking up.

I don't care. She put aside her busy work and covered her typewriter. *I don't care. I have Solomon.*

This was all for the good, she tried to tell herself. It was just as well that it was over.

I don't care if he misses me.

Solomon saw her car in the driveway. At least she had gotten home. That much was in order.

He entered the house and called her name. He heard a faint answer from somewhere on the second floor.

He climbed the stairs two at a time. He found her in their room, half reclining on the bed, staring at the wall. She turned to look at him, but didn't speak. Her face was sad. Contemplative.

"You okay?" he asked.

"I'm all right. Why?"

"I thought you were in some kind of trouble."

"Well, I'm not."

He had done it again. Failed again, for the second time that day. He had been so sure there was something wrong.

It looked as though she had melted into the bed. She was heavy and sodden. He realized that the heaviness was depression. It had something to do with a man. Not him. The other man.

He still felt something vibrating inside him. Something that alerted him to danger. She was all right, but the feeling persisted.

Danger. And she was depressed. He looked at her closely. She did not seem aware of him, but still she blocked her thoughts. He saw a mossy wall with water dripping down it. The strain of holding that wall in place was telling on her.

He couldn't understand his feeling. He didn't think her depression was the source of the danger. She wouldn't try anything stupid. He wished he could figure out what it was.

13

*H*E was riding in a police car. He had done it many times before, but this time he knew he was asleep.

Far ahead, a lone figure walked at the side of the road. They were in open country. There was no sidewalk, only a narrow shoulder.

The car quickly overtook the figure and now he could see that it was female. She wore pants and a fluffy jacket. Long dark hair rippled down her back. Beside him, the officer who was driving the car muttered, "Uh-oh."

The car slowed and the officer rolled down his window. "How about a lift? It's too late to be out alone at night, miss."

The girl turned with a smile. "Oh, thanks, but it's okay. I'm almost home."

"You're sure?"

"Thanks anyway."

The car drove on.

"You were right," said Solomon. The officer ignored him, because, of course, Solomon was not really there.

He looked back. They rounded a bend and the girl was no longer in sight. He thought he had seen the lights of another car, but he couldn't be sure.

It's happening, he told himself. There could be only one reason why he was having this dream. He tried to will himself into the girl's consciousness. Instead, he woke.

He could feel Libby next to him and see dim shapes in the room. There was always some light in their bedroom. It came from the street lamps outside.

Who is she?

It was going to happen. He knew it and he couldn't stop it. He had no idea who the girl was or where they had been. It was only a dark road. Things always looked different in the dark.

As he lay in bed, a photograph appeared before his eyes. He could tell from the quality that it was a newspaper picture. Now he could see all of the girl's face. It vanished before he could read the caption.

Vanished. He had glimpsed that word in the headline. That was all. He knew the whole story, and he couldn't stop it from happening.

He got out of bed, put on his bathrobe and slippers, and went downstairs to his study. He thought of calling Mike, but there was nothing he could do without more information.

He tried to clear his mind and wait, but nothing came to him. Nothing but Libby, asleep upstairs.

She was in danger, too. He knew it, but did not know from where the danger would come.

He leaned back in his chair. The study was dark, the windows gray rectangles. He could see the outline of the dracaena plant. He heard a car drive by on the street.

Then images began to pour into his mind. Again he saw Amy Basile, her eyes wide with terror above the chloroformed cloth. He saw her carried out to a car that stood with its trunk open, waiting for her. A man running back inside and leaving a note.

He saw a girl standing in shorts and a T-shirt, thumbing a ride. *Damn*, he thought, *why must they be so stupid?*

He saw another girl hitchhiking. A redhead this time. Dark red hair. A younger version of Libby.

His mind flashed ahead. He saw them arguing, the redhead and the man. She wanted to get out of the car. Solomon could almost see the man's face, but it was turned away from him. He thought there was something familiar about it. He willed the man to look at him.

Then he saw over the man's shoulder. The same girl had gotten away and was running down a grassy hillside. It was summer or early fall. She wore a light jacket. The man knocked her down with a football tackle. He could hear her scream.

The scene changed. She was tied to a bed, a narrow cot. He tried to see the house. It was a basement or cellar. A cot in a basement. Her mouth was taped shut, but he could still see her eyes. Blue eyes. He would never forget their expression. His own daughter had blue eyes.

A house. The man lived in a house, or at least had access to one. It would have to be isolated, because of the screams.

But where? Briefly he smelled alcohol and heard a quiet, satisfied laugh. A savage when he had been drinking. Solomon knew the girl was dead.

He sighed and rubbed his hand over his eyes. What had he accomplished? Exactly nothing. He could study the pictures of missing girls and tell what happened to them, but he hadn't seen the man. The killings would go on until they had him.

He did not return to bed for fear of disturbing Libby. Instead he lay on the sofa in his study. In the morning he got up at six o'clock and started the coffee.

An hour later she arrived in the kitchen, dressed for work. She seemed surprised to find him there. He was surprised to see her already dressed.

"I couldn't sleep," she said, checking her watch against the kitchen clock. She avoided looking at him.

He said, "I had trouble, too. Didn't want to bother you, so I came downstairs."

It was a ridiculous conversation. He counted the number of years they had been married. Four years, and they talked to each other like strangers.

"Are you going to eat?" he asked.

"Just coffee, thanks."

He poured his own cup and sat down with her at the table.

"Tell me something. Did you ever hitchhike?"

She stared at him in surprise. "Why?"

"I saw them last night. Some of the girls who have disappeared. Several of them were hitchhiking. I can't understand why girls do it. You keep reading about cases of rape and murder."

"What I can't understand," she said, "is how there can be so many rotten men. Blaming women for things like that is just a cop-out."

"It's not a matter of—"

"Why should a person have to live her whole life in accordance with what keeps her from becoming the victim of some creep?" Libby demanded. "That's not freedom. It's the ultimate of turning women into objects."

"I suppose that's true, but—"

"Do you know that you turn me into an object?"

Here we go again, he thought. Where had she gotten all this stuff?

"You do," she said. "You keep trying to tell me how I should be. Who I should be. You act as if I don't have any personality of my own, or any brains, or anything."

"That's the silliest thing I ever heard!" Solomon exclaimed.

"It's not. It's true. *Listen* to me sometimes, don't just tell me things. You think I've been seeing another man? Well, you're right, and do you know why? Because he treats me like a human being. He treats my opinions and ideas with respect."

Solomon's head reeled. He had suspected this, but he could not believe it was actually happening.

"I'm sorry," she murmured and got up from the table.

He still felt dazed. He watched her put on her coat and go out to her car. It was early yet, too early for work. Probably she was going to meet her lover for breakfast.

He wanted to tell her that she had just ruined him for the day, probably even longer. He couldn't possibly do any work now, but he didn't want to let her know that she had that much power over him.

Yes, he thought, she has power over me, and she thinks it's the other way around.

He went into his study, sat down at his desk, and called Mike Tarasco at home.

"I saw something happen last night," Solomon told him. "A girl, walking along a road. Some policeman offered her a ride, but she was almost home. And I know why I saw it."

"No reports so far," Mike replied. "Where was it, do you know?"

"That's the trouble. I don't know. Just an open road."

"What happened?"

"That's all." There was no point in mentioning the newspaper picture. "After that, I saw a lot of other things. The girls. I couldn't see the man."

"We got an i.d. on that body," said Mike. "Her name's Arletta Fowler. A year ago January she went shopping, never came home. A salesgirl saw her in Sears, and after that, nothing. It sounded like a runaway case."

"Her family didn't think she ran away."

"No. They pasted up fliers all over the place. Sometimes families are right about things like that." Mike sounded miserable.

"Even if you'd looked for her, you wouldn't have found her."

"Maybe you could."

"I doubt it." Solomon thought of Libby and what she had just handed him. Of course that hadn't been the case a year ago. "It would have been too late," he muttered.

"What are you doing today?"

"I—" He tried to think, and then he remembered. "That Knapp kid. There's a memorial service. She wants me to come."

He didn't want to go. He didn't want to do anything but stay at home in his study. His haven. But he couldn't let Iris down.

Why the hell not? he asked himself.

Because he just couldn't. And it might be good for him to get away from home for a while.

He wondered if Mike was going back to the woods, but he didn't want to ask. They had combed it yesterday on his advice and found nothing. He still thought there was another grave, but maybe he was wrong.

"Sorry I can't give you any more," he said.

"Take it easy, Sol. We'll just plod along."

"I'll let you know if I get something."

But he wouldn't get anything. And if he did, he wouldn't know whether it was right.

All because of Libby. He should have left well enough alone after Jayne. He had wanted love and companionship, but it always seemed to turn sour.

All you needed, he thought, leaning back in his chair, was a disturbed personality, a few slaps in the face like the ones he had had, and you could almost understand why a man would go around murdering women.

14

"You've got to make him stop," Frances Basile pleaded when Mike Tarasco met her at the hospital. "Make him stop. He's killing us, just the way he killed her."

Mike put his arm around the distraught woman's shoulders and led her into the sun room. "Tell me what happened."

"He called again last night. He asked if we found her yet. He wouldn't tell us anything. After he hung up, that's when Joe had the heart attack. Please make him stop, Mr. Tarasco. He keeps calling."

"He gets a kick out of talking to you. Hearing your voices," Mike said. "We're trying to find him, believe me. I'm sorry you have to be troubled with a thing like that. At least we have the kidnapper. How's your husband doing?"

"They said he'll be all right, but I don't know. If this goes on..."

"It won't go on. We're bound to catch the guy. Most of these cranks aren't too long on brains. He'll trip himself up."

"Are you sure he's a crank?" she asked.

"Well, he's not the kidnapper. We've got a confession on that," Mike reminded her.

"I just thought— He knew about the chloroform. I thought he might be a friend, or something."

"We're checking on that. The guy we have in custody doesn't talk much, but we'll get to him."

"I hope so."

"You can bet on it." He patted her back. "We've got a tape of the phone call, of course. It'll help in voice identification." A little white lie to make her feel better. Any identification was useless without a suspect.

"My husband," the woman began reluctantly, "wants you to ask that psychic about it. The one you brought to our house. I don't know what good it's going to do, but he said that. It was just before he had the attack."

"You understand," Mike replied, "Mr. Thayer donates his services. I hate to ask him about a thing like that, when there are so many—"

"*Please*? He said it just before—"

"Yes, I know. Just before he had the attack." Mike supposed she thought of it as something like a last request.

"I'll mention it to him." He started to ease himself away.

"I'd appreciate it," Mrs. Basile said. Then she asked, "What about...her? You haven't told us anything."

"We're still working on that. The guy was pretty whacked out on drugs. He couldn't remember straight. Told us a lot of different things."

She reached for his hand. "I'm sorry to bother you, Mr. Tarasco. It's just that I need somebody to talk to."

"Right, I understand." He gave her hand a squeeze. "Call me any time. If I'm not there, I'll get right back to you."

Mike drove to his office, arriving early, and telephoned Solomon.

"Am I interrupting anything?" he asked.

"What would you be interrupting?"

"I thought you had your clients in the morning. You sounded busy."

"Not busy. Just—" Solomon clamped his jaws together. Mike was a good friend, but maybe no friend was good enough for him to spill his guts about Libby. "Just thinking."

"We've got another problem. Not as bad as the kidnapping, but it's the last straw for the Basiles. There's this guy who keeps calling them in the middle of the night. He pretends to be the kidnapper and talks about their daughter. It got so bad, Joe had a heart attack last night. He's in the hospital."

"I'm sorry to hear that." Once again Solomon was brought up short by the realization that other people had it worse than he did.

"Why do you think he's pretending?" he asked.

"Now, Sol, you know why. If a guy confesses, that's it, as far as the investigation goes."

"What if three guys confess? How do you choose which one?"

"Let's not get into that right now. You and I just

aren't going to agree on this. Maybe you'll prove me wrong. Do you think you can help? The Basiles are pretty insistent. Want to hear a tape of the man's voice?"

"I'd love to," Solomon said dryly. "Maybe before that service this afternoon. How's twelve-thirty?"

Twelve-thirty was fine with Mike. Solomon remained at his desk, trying to clear his mind. He had no clients scheduled for that morning. He could spend the time on the Basile case. Both cases, the telephone caller and the kidnapper. He tried not to think about Libby.

At noon he changed into a suit for the memorial service and then drove to the police station. Mike was not there. He found Farley O'Brien at his desk, frowning over a tape recorder.

"Mike had to go out for a while," Farley explained. "He says you know about this. Did you have lunch?"

Solomon realized that lunch had slipped his mind. Farley sent out for two pastrami sandwiches and coffee.

He handed Solomon a set of earphones. "Helps you concentrate better," he said. "They're good phones. They don't distort the sound."

"Even telephones give you some distortion." Solomon adjusted the earphones and started the tape.

It was the first call, the one in which the Basiles were informed of their daughter's death by chloroform. He listened, feeling the hair rise at the back of his neck, and then he turned off the machine.

"This is the kidnapper," he said.

Farley stared at him in confusion. "What about Redfield?"

"I don't know, but I know this is the voice of the kidnapper. You didn't even need me to tell you that. He knew about the chloroform."

"Yeah, I heard she made that point, too," said Farley.

"Who did?"

"Basile. What do you want us to do, go on investigating? Redfield confessed."

"There's no point in prosecuting him for a crime he didn't commit. Even if he says he did," replied Solomon.

Farley wailed, "We've got no *proof* there was somebody else, and what we have got is a confession."

Solomon shrugged. "If I were you, I'd try a different tack. Find out why he confessed."

"He'll say it's because he did it."

"Look, you told me the man's an addict. Won't they often do anything for drugs?"

Farley dropped his head into his hand. "But that? His whole life?"

"What kind of life do you think he has, if he's an addict? They live for drugs. For them, that *is* life. And they only live from day to day anyhow."

"Fix to fix," O'Brien corrected him. "I don't know, Solomon. As far as the department's concerned, we've got him. Mike and I would have to investigate on our own, and we don't know where to start."

"Unfortunately," said Solomon, "I don't either."

He put the earphones back on his head and restarted the tape.

He began to get a clearer picture. It was an educated man, but sick. A psychopath. He was pretending to be something he wasn't. As a psychopath, he was unscrupulous, clever, and manipulative. He could fool anybody and everybody. They took him for what he pretended to be.

He felt another horrid chill as he remembered the impressions he had gotten from Libby's gold pen. He kept that part of it to himself and told the rest to Farley.

"Yeah, but what does he look like?" asked Farley. "What does he do? Where is he?"

Solomon had to admit he didn't know.

"It's here somewhere." He tapped his head. "I can feel it. It's here, like a word on the tip of the tongue."

"All of it?"

"Maybe not all, but more than I've come up with." He struggled to think, knowing he couldn't force it. His mind kept returning to Libby. It occurred to him that maybe *she* was not in danger. Maybe the danger was to him, because of her. The danger of losing her.

Why did he care so much? She was making him crazy. Maybe he would be better off alone. It would be a serene and tranquil life. Maybe he needed that.

"Hey, I've got to go," he said. "I'm already late."

Maybe somebody like Iris. No, he didn't want to

get involved again. No more young wives who admired him for a while and then wanted out, driving him crazy in the process.

"I'll be working on it," he told Farley and went out to his car. He got in behind the wheel and inserted the key. Before he had a chance to turn it, his hand seemed to freeze.

The ignition switch, the wheel, the parking lot, all disappeared. Instead of sitting, he stood half-crouched, alert and listening, in an entirely different place.

He recognized the place. He was in the living room of Iris Knapp's apartment. He stood next to the television set, facing into the room. On his right was the front door, and in the corner, her massive sofa. Straight ahead was the row of three high windows filled with hanging plants. Beyond them he could see the grassy lawn and a pair of sneakered feet walking by.

All this, he noticed in an instant. He didn't have to study the room, because he knew it.

At the same time, he knew that he didn't know it, and that he shouldn't be there.

He heard footsteps approaching the door, coming down the stairs from outside.

It was too early. It must be someone else. He would have to hide or get out. Quickly!

But how? There was only the one door. The windows were too high. He could never climb up to them fast enough and fight his way through the hanging plants.

He looked about for a closet. He would have to

hide and then try to sneak out when he could. But that was impossible. The apartment was too small to slip past whoever was coming. He was trapped.

Solomon jerked himself awake.
He called it that, although he had not been asleep. The thing he had experienced was far more vivid and immediate than a dream. He still felt suffocated. Trapped and desperate.

He knew what it was. They did it all the time. They watched for some notice of a funeral service, and then they would go and rob the family's home. He knew someone was there now, or would be soon. And he had been in that person's mind, hearing Iris come home after the service.

Why would she be alone? he wondered. How could they do that to her? But the footsteps had been a single pair of feet.

He had no idea how long the service would last. Probably not very long. How much could you say about a four-year-old child?

And he should be there, but this was more important. He turned on his engine and shifted into reverse. He looked over at the police station. It would have been logical to go and tell Farley, but he had been wrong so often lately. He knew he was right about this. It felt right, but he had felt right about that other grave in the woods, too.

And the voice on the tape. Maybe he was wrong.
He caught himself going through a red light. He looked back. There were no police cars, and luckily he had not collided with anyone. He would have to

watch himself, slow down to thirty miles an hour.

He ticked off the streets, feeling that he was zeroing in on a target. This was the last one. He made a right turn and drove down a hill to the complex where she lived. He left his car without bothering to park it, dashed around the corner of the end building and past two entrances to Number 8. Down a flight of steps to a tiny foyer with two doors marked respectively *A* and *B*. He knocked on *B*.

No sound came from inside. She wasn't back yet. Or maybe she was back and already dead, or unconscious, or bound and gagged. He called through the door, "Mrs. Knapp? Iris!"

He tested the knob. The door moved slightly but did not open. He could see a latch that he thought was the snaplock. He stood back, wondering whether he could break it down. Then he remembered the plastic trick. Fumbling in his wallet, he pulled out an Exxon card.

Footsteps sounded on the concrete walk outside. He stopped and looked around in alarm. The footsteps passed on by the entrance and faded away.

They could haul him in for trespassing, if not for breaking and entering. And what if there was no one inside? His vision had been clear enough, but there was no date on it. It might have been meant for another time, sometime in the future.

Still, he couldn't take a chance. The snaplock itself meant danger. Iris had told him, when he worried about her security, that whether she was in or out, she always bolted the door.

With his card, he jimmied the latch out of the way

and swung open the door. He stood surveying the living room. It was peaceful, quiet, and empty, with sunlight shining through the hanging plants and falling in patches on the floor.

"Iris?"

Still there was only silence, but for him it was alive. He felt a ripple somewhere in all that peace. A kind of tension. A breath held behind a half-closed door.

He rubbed the back of his neck. It felt still and tight. His lungs strained from an unconsciously held breath.

The bedroom. At that moment he saw a large *R*. Ritchie? No, he was confusing things again.

An *R* and an *M*. Or was it *N*? And something dark, with ragged edges. When he recognized it, he felt suffocated. It was the hole they had dug in the woods, where they found the body.

He started down the short hallway toward the bedroom. It occurred to him to warn the intruder, to announce that he knew he was there, rather than surprise him. The man might be armed.

"You may as well come on out," he said, and paused for a response. He heard nothing, but felt a wary silence. Waiting fear. A readiness.

"Whatever you do," he went on, "I can track you down. I already know something about you and I can find out the rest."

He stopped and listened again. He heard a rustle. Then the faint creak of a door.

He barely had time to register the footfall when a figure hurtled toward him. Solomon dodged to one side, put out his foot, and caught the figure low on the shins.

A blurred, featureless face looked up at him. After an instant of total shock, Solomon realized that it was a stocking mask.

He had knocked the intruder to a sprawl, but the man was evidently younger, and lithe. He rolled over and jumped to his feet. His fist aimed for Solomon's belly.

Solomon gasped, trying to draw a breath. He felt the wall's cold plaster against his back and slumped forward, but caught himself from falling. He strained for air. His head was growing light. Finally he managed a small breath. He clutched at his diaphragm, where the man had hit him.

He heard a door slam. The outside door. Still doubled over, he made his way to the sofa.

Shouldn't have been so stupid, he thought. Should have gotten the police. But he hadn't been sure that he was right. Didn't believe in himself anymore. All her fault, damn it.

He closed his eyes and saw the stocking mask slip into another house. A kitchen. He recognized that, too. The Basile home.

The stocking mask gave the man a face without features. A face with no identity, no personality. It seemed to Solomon that that was the man himself.

Before he could reflect on it, he heard a refrigerator door open. An arm shot out. He saw the girl's heart-shaped face tipped back and the white cloth over her mouth. Her wide, terrified eyes. Then she slid down toward the floor.

He tried to get up. To look for a telephone. A pain shot through his gut.

I was right, he thought triumphantly.

What difference did it make? He was going to die here of internal hemorrhaging.

He would not let himself die now, before he had a chance to tell Mike. He tried again to stand. He felt as though something would rip apart if he moved.

Footsteps scraped on the stairs. He heard the jingle of keys. He tried to draw a breath to announce his presence. By the time he discovered he couldn't, she had the door open.

"Mr. Thayer!"

"Call," he gasped, "police."

"What happened?"

"Burglar."

"Are you all right?"

"Damn it," he said as his lungs finally filled, "will you call the police?"

She looked as though he had struck her, but she set down her handbag and picked up the phone.

He gave her the number. "Ask for Mike Tarasco," he said. "If he's not there, Farley O'Brien."

He shouldn't have talked to her like that. He could see how hurt she was, and of course she couldn't have known what happened. She was still finding her way, and he had let his impatience overcome him.

He realized that he did it to Libby, too, maybe more times than he cared to acknowledge.

She hung up the phone. Without looking at him, she said, "They're on their way."

"Sorry I yelled," he told her gruffly. "The guy

punched me out, and—hell, it was too late to catch him anyway."

"That's okay." She walked over and stood in front of him. "Are you hurt?"

"Not anymore. But you are, and I'm sorry." He felt awkward. The world of apology was alien to him. But while he was at it, he apologized for missing the service, too.

"I was on my way," he explained, "when I got the feeling somebody was here, and you might be coming in. Hey, why are you alone?"

"My parents had to get back," she said. "Dad doesn't like driving after dark."

He wondered if he would have done better than that for Sybil. He hoped it would never happen to Sybil.

"What about the boy's father?"

"I don't know where he is, and anyway, I doubt if he's changed. It's okay, Mr. Thayer. And thank you for coming. Here, I mean."

She had gone back to calling him Mr. Thayer. She saw him as a much older man.

"Glad to do it. And I think we might be on to something, if I can get them to believe me."

"The police?"

"Yes. It might help to straighten out one of their cases, but again, it might confuse it more. *I'm* very confused about what I saw. Anyway, at least you're safe. That's what counts."

15

"WHAT was it?" asked Mike. "A white or a black man?"

"I told you, he wore a stocking mask. No, wait. His hands. A black man." It was a dark fist that had shot out at him. Dark and shiny. Or was it a glove?

Mike was busy writing.

"Cross that out," Solomon told him. "I don't know."

"Okay, we'll stick with what you do know. About six feet, maybe a hundred eighty pounds, navy sweats, blue and white sneakers."

"Running shoes. They were running shoes."

"You're sure?"

"Pretty sure." Solomon did not know much about athletic footwear, but he thought that was what they were. It figured, with the sweats. All designed for agility and a quick getaway.

"Mike," he said, "I want to talk to you."

Mike was reading over his notes. "Sure. Talk."

Solomon glanced at Iris Knapp, who sat huddled on the sofa, trying to recover from the shock piled upon tragedy. It would have to wait until they were out of there.

"Okay, that's it?" Mike asked.

"All for now," Solomon replied.

Mike turned to Iris. "You don't know anybody who might have a key?"

"No, I don't. Nobody except the building super."

"Did you have your lock changed when you moved in?"

Her voice dropped. "No, I didn't."

"Always should, when you take a new apartment. Some people throw their keys around like confetti. And get it done now."

"Of course," she said.

"Now."

Mike waited while she telephoned a locksmith. When he was assured that the locksmith would be there in ten minutes, he and Solomon left.

The sun was low but still bright, shining with a yellow intensity and actually managing to give off warmth. It was almost a spring day.

"What did you want to tell me?" Mike asked as they walked toward the parking lot.

"That man, the burglar."

"What about him?"

"I'm not sure, but I felt he had something to do with the kidnapping."

Mike rolled his eyes and muttered an expletive. "Don't give me that."

This case, Solomon reflected, marked the first time Mike had ever doubted him.

"Can't blame you," Solomon told his friend, "after my record the last few days, but you ought to give it a chance. What good does it do to close your mind?"

"Look," said Mike, "I could go for a cup of coffee. How about you?"

"Not now. I—" Solomon stopped walking. He turned his face to the sun, but his eyes were tightly closed.

"I felt him. I felt the pain inside him." He had not realized it at the time, but he was feeling it now.

"Who, the intruder?"

"It's all connected," Solomon went on. "The man. I don't know what he wanted. Not her. Not that time. Just to get inside her home, maybe. Did you notice she has long hair?"

"Who?"

"Iris. It's all connected. The Basile girl. The body you found near the landfill. The others. There's a grave. Two together."

"Sol, we looked for that grave."

The images were pounding at him. The pain left him feeling as though he had been hit by a truck. He was in no condition to drive home.

They walked down a flight of steps to the swimming pool. It was drained and covered for the winter. On the far side, a young woman pushed a baby carriage, trailed by a child on a tricycle.

Solomon paced the walk by the pool, still trying to make sense of the things that flashed through his brain.

"He's free," he said. "Not Redfield. The kidnapper's free." He saw the *R* again. And tawny grasses rippling in a wind. It had something to do with childhood. His childhood. The killer's.

"Oh my God."

"What is it?" asked Mike.

"The pain. The *pain*. He's terrified. Trying to keep himself together. I see this—thing—flying apart. A storm. His whole personality." Solomon pressed his hands to his head.

"You know something?" said Mike. "You're nuts."

"No. No, he is. He hurts. It's a storm inside him. He has to let it out. Has to kill."

"What the hell for?"

"It's the only way he can hold together. Keep going. As a person."

"Like a safety valve."

Solomon did not answer.

"Hell," said Mike, "I'll never understand these things. All I know is, I gotta pick up the pieces."

Solomon barely heard him. He was caught up in the man's inner storm, feeling the anguish, the splintering, the rage.

"He can't," he went on, "can't face it. He has to get out. Invent another—"

"What are you talking about?"

"Another— He believes, really believes, it's someone else."

"How do you know all this?"

"Bobby Redfield. The killer wants to believe it's Bobby Redfield. Mike, I just feel these things."

"I know you do."

Mike also knew that, like anyone else, Solomon

could be wrong sometimes, and obviously this was one of those times. It was hard to imagine why Redfield would have borrowed all that trouble.

"Wait a minute," said Solomon. "I'm getting more. About the killings."

He didn't want more. It made him sick, but he couldn't stop it.

"Awe full," he said.

Awful and full of awe.

"A ritual." He stared at the green tarp over the swimming pool, at the sunlight on the grass.

"Not just a joy killing. Sometimes he keeps them alive for a while."

"For what?"

"Till he's finished."

"Oh."

"Or another comes along." And another had come along last night. He had seen it.

"Then," he went on, "for him, it's almost—almost like a sacrifice. A union with mother death."

He heard Mike mutter, "You lost me."

More visions came. He saw the eyes, only the eyes. He saw the lust in them.

And then the hands. He saw what the man was doing.

"Stop it!" he cried.

"What?" asked Mike.

"Stop them coming! I don't want to see anymore."

"Maybe you have to. To understand."

Solomon looked around him at the unreal day. At the young mother across the pool. She had sat down on a bench and was watching him. A stick figure.

And Mike. A cardboard statue.

The evergreen shrubbery. The grass. Life was coming back to the grass and the sun still shone on it, but for him it was gone. The horror had washed it away and the sunlight was gone. Destroyed.

"The sickness. It goes beyond all bounds."

"What is it?" asked Mike. "Tell me."

"It's evil, the things he does. It makes—everything—"

"Evil?" said Mike. "That's a theological word. You're not going to pass judgment on a sick person, are you? It's a sickness."

"I know, I know. I don't mean to be judgmental. It's only the way it hits me. It makes me feel—all this sunshine—as if it doesn't belong. As if the sun turned black."

16

LIBBY combed her dark red hair in the rest room at the office. In a few minutes, she would be seeing Neale again. It had happened. He had finally called and she was to meet him after work.

Her nerves were strung out with an odd mixture of elation, guilt, and fear.

The memory of that morning made her cringe. She never should have told Solomon she was seeing another man. It was too cruel.

She ought to go home now, instead of this, but she was afraid to face him. She was also afraid of losing Neale. She felt confused, taut, ready to snap.

It's my fault, she thought. I should have—shouldn't have...

Maybe she should have learned to keep her mouth shut. To take what was thrown at her, without having to answer back.

When she left the office and saw Neale waiting for her, the guilt and fear abated. She was glad she had made this decision.

"Hi," he said, smiling as he came toward her. He

wrapped his arm around hers and took her hand.

She smiled back. "You've been busy."

"I sure have. What about you?"

As if it were he who had been waiting for her call, instead of the other way around.

She asked, "What are you working on, the Redfield case?"

He shrugged. "Yes and no. There's not much to work on. After all, the man confessed. Anyway, I shouldn't be talking about it. What would you like to do, have a drink somewhere?"

She agreed, but didn't like the sound of it. One quick drink, and he would send her on her way. It must have meant he wasn't really serious about her. That she was just a plaything.

Panic choked her. It had to be more than that!

He said, "The Spanish place has a bar, doesn't it?"

"Aranho's? Yes, it does. Anyway, Neale, it's Portuguese."

"So, what's the difference?"

"I guess there isn't much. Anyway, I already know what I want. A Margarita."

"You really like those things, don't you?"

"Yes, and I never had one before that first lunch of ours."

Aranho's cocktail lounge was decorated like a cave, or more probably, a wine cellar. They took a table in a small, darkened booth. She ordered her Margarita, and he, a double scotch.

She must have looked startled. He grinned and explained, "It's been a tough day. I have to unwind."

"Why, what happened?"

"Just—things. For a while, I thought I wouldn't get a chance to see you."

A waitress brought their drinks. Neale gulped down half his scotch and then seemed to relax.

"How can you do that?" Libby asked.

"Do what?"

"Drink it like that. Doesn't it burn your throat?"

"You get used to it. My throat's probably pickled by now."

"Do you drink a lot?"

"Sometimes, when things pile up. Why?"

She really didn't know him very well. Not nearly as well as she wished.

"I just wondered. It's not very healthy, you know."

"It isn't. I guess I'm a weak person. In fact, I know I am."

"Everybody has their weaknesses. Maybe you take on more than you can handle," she said, thinking of Bobby Redfield.

"Maybe."

She scratched at a stain on the tablecloth. "We had a sort of scene the other night. My husband found that pen you gave me."

"The what?"

"That gold pen. It must have fallen out of my purse. I told him I got it from somebody at the office."

"Why not?"

"I don't think he believed me. But he can't prove anything."

"There's nothing to prove. It's just a pen. Why make a fuss about it?"

She was relieved to hear that it meant nothing and embarrassed at having brought it up. She wished she would learn to feel at ease with him.

Neale ordered another scotch and drank it quickly.

"You don't feel like eating right now, do you?" he asked.

She didn't, especially when he put it that way. He suggested that they pick up some food and go to his place.

At least he was not ready to end the evening. It made her glad, but at the same time, she felt a strange reluctance. Maybe this was moving faster than she wanted.

But maybe it was time to stop pussyfooting and do something definite about her situation. Maybe she herself had already taken the first step this morning in her argument with Solomon.

"What about my car?" she asked.

"We'll pick it up later, okay? Come on."

Neale lived on the northeast edge of Fairmont Park, away from the elegant homes farther west. His house was small, with a steep, wooded hill rising to one side and an empty lot on the other. She thought, *How desolate*. She had never seen a house in the middle of a city look so alone.

He seemed to read her thoughts. Nodding toward the empty lot, he explained, "There was a fire there a couple of years ago. I don't know why they never rebuilt, but it makes it nice and private."

"I think it's kind of spooky. Don't you get nervous here all by yourself?"

"What's to get nervous about?"

"I suppose it helps, being a man."

He led her up the walk and unlocked the front door. She felt a moment of misgiving and wondered what she was doing there. As soon as he turned on a light, she was reassured. The house was comfortably furnished, and its very smallness gave it a cozy feeling.

"What's that?"

He had turned on a lamp in the living room. In one corner stood a glass cabinet filled with handguns, everything from elaborate dueling pistols to Saturday night specials.

"I collect those," he said. "Anything wrong?"

"I'll never understand men."

"Some people collect stamps. Why, does it bother you?"

"A little."

"Look at it this way, Libby. In my work, I deal with a lot of criminals. They can be volatile and irrational. If I lose a case and they get convicted, there are always some who'll hold it against me. This is my insurance against dissatisfied clients."

"Why do you need so many?"

"Because I collect them. It's a hobby."

He helped her remove her coat and took it to a closet in the hallway.

"I didn't know criminal lawyers were in so much danger," she said.

"It depends on the type of client."

"Well, why do you do it?"

"I love it. And you have to remember something. They're not all guilty. Even if they are, somebody has to help them."

"Well, that's true." She knew they were all entitled

to counsel. She would want it herself, if she were ever arrested.

"Shouldn't we do something with the steak?" she asked.

"We'll put it in the fridge for now." He took the grocery bag into the kitchen and stored the food. Then he turned to her, smiling. "Want another drink?"

"I don't think so, thank you."

"I'll have one, if you don't mind."

He kept bottles of liquor on his kitchen counter. As he poured another large scotch, she again had qualms. Maybe this was not a good day to be here. She had never seen him drink so much before.

"Do you have any soda?" she asked, thinking she would join him with a glass of something.

"Ginger ale under the counter. You'll need ice."

She fixed her drink and they went into the living room. She sat on the sofa next to a pile of newspapers. He removed the papers and took the seat beside her.

"We could get comfortable," he proposed. "We could go up to my bed. It might be more comfortable."

"Well...maybe later. Oh, could I use your bathroom?"

"Of course. Right at the top of the stairs."

She set down her drink and climbed up to a darkened second floor. In the glow from downstairs, she could make out the bathroom. She groped for a light.

As soon as it went on, she noticed something long, black, and filmy draped over the laundry hamper. A very revealing nightgown, or two halves of one, with bowties to secure it at the waist.

Oh, no. Oh, no.

She hurried to finish what she had come for, straightened her hair, and went back downstairs.

"Do you have a girl friend?" she asked.

"What, the gown? Yes, I did have someone. Nothing serious. She kept saying she'd come back and collect it, so I left it there."

Right where she had dropped it? Really?

"Doesn't it get in your way?"

"A little thing like that?"

"Maybe you like to be reminded of her."

He laughed and held out his arm. "Come here."

She picked up her drink and sat down. He dropped his arm. She had not wanted to go to him when he called her like that, as though she were a dog.

He asked, "Are you jealous?"

"No, I was just surprised."

"Did you think I was some kind of pervert, or something?"

She looked at him over her glass. "I assumed it belonged to a woman, but—how come you don't put it away in a drawer?"

"Because she keeps saying she's coming back for it."

He swallowed the last of his drink and went out to the kitchen. He was going to pour another. She wondered again if she should leave.

Do I love him? she asked herself. Am I scared because of Solomon, or what?

He came back empty-handed.

"That poor guy," he said. "Do you know he's sick?"

"Who?"

"Bobby Redfield, who else? The man who kidnapped that girl."

"Well, I guess it's not a very normal thing to do."

"He's sick. They had to put him in a home when he was a kid."

"What sort of home?"

"For kids whose parents couldn't handle them. How do you like that? People have kids who never ask to be born, and then they don't want to raise them."

She stared at the floor. She felt that way, too. All the unwanted children in the world, and she couldn't have any.

"After that, some other people adopted him," Neale went on, "but by then it was too late. Nobody ever really tried to help him. Nobody cared. His own parents didn't care."

"If I had a child," she said, "I'd care very much. That's part of having children, loving them no matter what. If you can't do that, you shouldn't have them."

She didn't think he was listening. He stared ahead, and his eyes seemed glazed.

"He used to wake up screaming," Neale said.

"Redfield?"

"In the home. At night he'd get these awful terrors, not quite nightmares, and he'd wake up screaming. He kept thinking about death. All the time."

"Do you mean he was afraid of dying?"

"Not really. He just thought about it. He used to pretend he was going to the electric chair."

"How horrible! I wonder why. Because his parents didn't want him?"

"That probably had something to do with it, but there must have been more."

"Like what?"

"There was something—a kind of—like a sickness inside him. For a long time, he didn't know. It just kept growing."

"A tumor?"

"No," said Neale in disgust. "Something—I don't know how to describe it. It was something he couldn't understand."

"Well," she said, "I wish he'd told somebody."

"He didn't know. How could he tell anyone? He didn't know what it was."

"Yes, but maybe they could have helped him, and he wouldn't have killed that poor girl."

"She wasn't the first one, either."

Libby felt jolted. "Did he tell you that, too?"

"Not exactly. I just happen to know. I understand him pretty well."

"You must be some super attorney."

"He never meant to kill her, the first one. I don't think he meant to kill any of them. He couldn't help himself. There was a little boy, too, but that was different."

"How was it—" Her mouth suddenly felt dry. "How was it different?"

"That wasn't supposed to be a death. It was only—there was something he missed. Something innocent."

She thought he was getting maudlin, and it embarrassed her. "Neale, I think you've been drinking too much."

"He missed it. He missed being a boy. He wanted to get back there, but—he never meant to kill the kid."

"You don't mean that Knapp boy."

"I don't know what I mean."

Neale settled back on the sofa. His mouth was set in a firm line, but she thought his eyes looked bright and rather damp.

17

"Is he a friend of yours?" she asked. "A personal friend?"

"More than that."

"Bobby Redfield?"

He stared at her and blinked. Then he said slowly, "Bobby Redfield."

She felt the earth fall away from under her. He sounded as though he hadn't even been thinking of Bobby Redfield. She looked down into the abyss and didn't want to contemplate it.

"I just thought," she said weakly, "I mean, you seemed so emotionally involved."

"Sometimes I do that, unfortunately."

"My husband does it, too." She began to chatter. "Well, sometimes he can't help it, because he feels what the person is feeling. But other times, if he's looking for a missing child, for instance, he'll be right in there with the parents."

He nodded understandingly.

"Anyway," she said, "I thought you weren't supposed to talk to me about the case."

"I probably shouldn't, but I thought I could trust you."

"Oh, you can! I'll just listen and forget all about it. I know it sometimes helps to clarify things in your own mind, if you can talk about it."

Still chattering. The entire episode disturbed her. Had he really been talking about Bobby Redfield? She had never known a lawyer to get teary over a client's background, however pitiful it might have been. Maybe it was the alcohol that stirred his emotions.

"Does he talk about the kidnapping?" she ventured.

Neale didn't answer. He bent and untied his shoes.

"Maybe I should go home," she said. "Solomon might be worried."

"You just got here."

"But I—"

"We didn't eat yet. Don't you want to eat?"

"Maybe we could start on that now?"

"In a little while. I'm not ready." He slipped off his shoes. He had said nothing more about bed. Maybe he was only getting comfortable.

She was comfortable, too, right where she was. She hated the thought of going out into the cold and having to drive herself home. She hated, perhaps more than anything, the inevitable scene with Solomon.

She looked around the room, trying to think of something to say. She didn't want to talk about the guns, or the nightgown upstairs.

"How long have you lived here?" she asked.
"Couple of years."
"It really is a nice place. I'd like to see it in the daytime."
"You can, if you spend the night."
"You're joking, of course. How could I spend the night without Solomon knowing?"
"Would he be able to find out where you are?" he asked.
"Maybe."

She knew he didn't believe it. He didn't know what Solomon could do. She took another drink of ginger ale. It was flat and watery.

"Can I ask you one question?"
"About?"
"The Redfield case. Then I'll drop it."

Again he said nothing. She assumed he was waiting for the question.

"Do you think the girl is dead?"
"Why do you want to know that?" he asked.
"I think everybody wants to know. She's just a young girl. A child. I wondered if he might have told you anything."
"Well," said Neale, "he might have."

It was undoubtedly privileged information. She kept silent, but hoped he would go on.

Finally he suggested, "Why don't you ask your husband?"

"He doesn't know. I thought it would be so wonderful if he could find her, but he can't."

"He probably won't."
"How do you know?"

"She's probably well hidden."

Was he assuming, or did he know? Again it sounded as though he were more involved than he claimed to be.

"Did Redfield do it alone?" she asked.

"All alone."

"But if he confessed to the crime, why doesn't he tell you where she is?"

"He doesn't know. He forgot. But she's dead. That's what he does. He kills them."

"You make it sound like a routine."

"Well, he's a sick person. I told you that, didn't I? He has this—he told me he has a fantasy about dead girls. It's horrible. He's really sick."

She had an inkling of what kind of fantasy he meant.

"So he collects them," Neale went on. "One by one, and does his thing with them."

"But I didn't hear of any other kidnappings."

"Hitchhikers. Runaways. The Basile girl was the first from around here. I'm afraid of what that means."

"Why? What does it mean?"

"Isn't it obvious? He's getting more reckless. I'm afraid it means—he's losing control."

"It seems to me, he must have already lost control," she said. "But what is it? What's wrong with him?"

"I told you, he's sick."

"I don't understand."

"What don't you understand?"

"What makes a person like that?"

"I couldn't tell you. He was— I already said there was something inside him. Something not quite right. He was always—difficult. They had trouble with him. Couldn't handle him. That made it worse. Finally they put him away."

Should have kept him there, she thought.

"Do you mean he was born sick?"

"I don't know," said Neale. "He didn't know, when he was little. I told you that, didn't I? He thought he was just like other kids. He played with other kids, he went to school. But there was something there. Something that wasn't quite right. It bothered him sometimes. He didn't know what it was. Other times it scared him."

"What was it?"

Neale did not answer immediately. He gazed at the floor, at his stockinged feet.

"The sickness, whatever it is," he said after a while. "You called it a tumor. Maybe it is sort of like that, except you can't see it. He just knew he wasn't right inside, but he didn't know what to do about it. He didn't know how to make it stop hurting."

"If it was that bad, why couldn't he tell somebody? His parents?"

"His parents! That's a laugh. All they cared about was the hard time he gave them."

"I had parents like that," she said.

"Maybe it's natural, I don't know. I never had kids."

"But it shouldn't be that way. It's like Solomon. He just wants me to behave his way. He doesn't stop and think that I'm me, not him. I guess I got myself into that. When we were first married, I didn't know any better. I just wanted approval."

"Well, it certainly didn't help—him," Neale went on. "It didn't help one bit. All he knew was, he couldn't cope. He seemed to clash instead, and that made it worse. The thing inside got bigger and angrier. And finally, the only thing he could do was kill. The only thing that meant anything was death."

She put her hand to her throat. "How horrible. And he told you all that?"

"Most of it. But I know him. I know what he was going through."

"Why does he have to kill? I don't understand. What does he want?"

"Peace."

"Peace?"

"From the torment."

"But that's terrible. Why should somebody be born like that?"

"I don't know how much of it he was born with."

"He must have talked to you an awful lot."

"All my life."

"What?"

"I mean—about all *his* life. He told me, for instance, how he used to look at skin pictures."

"What?"

"Magazines."

"Pornography?"

"You really are awfully naive, aren't you?" he said.

"I don't think so. I knew what you meant."

"Things like that. All those sex things. But sex always meant death."

He had made a slip with that "all my life." She didn't see how he could have known Bobby Redfield all his life. Aside from the fact that Neale was a good ten years older, the newspaper said Redfield had grown up in Fairmont Park, whereas Neale had lived in Roscoe and then Trenton.

It was possible. It had to be, but she was afraid he was lying about something. He was drunk, and it frightened her.

"I really ought to go home," she said again.

He reached out and caught her wrist. "Not yet. Don't go yet. I need you here. This is a bad time for me."

Solomon tried to settle down, but he couldn't. Too much was going on. Mike had gotten a radio call and rushed off somewhere. He hadn't said anything, but again Solomon saw the grave with two bodies in it.

He had gone home to find himself alone. At the time she usually drove in, the house was quiet. She wasn't coming. He knew that.

Another man, he thought as he walked through the living room, pounding the heels of his hands together.

A younger man. How stupid could he have been? He was in his prime when she married him. Now he was passing it, and she was just entering hers.

Damn.

The telephone rang. He took quick strides into his

study. He knew it wouldn't be Libby.

"Sol?"

"Yes, Mike."

"Gotta hand it to you, fella."

"You found it."

"Yup. Right in that woods, but way back. Near the back of the landfill. I was counting on the dog."

"They're not infallible. Neither am I."

"You were right about the two of them. One on top of the other. They were buried at different times."

"Right."

"Well, I thought you'd want to know."

"Wait."

Mike waited.

"She's cold," said Solomon.

"Who?"

"Basile."

"Hey, look—"

"She's cold and she's having trouble breathing. Mike, can you come over?"

"I guess so."

"Just come."

Mike sighed, disconnected the line, and thought of calling his family. He changed his mind. He had told them not to expect him anyway, when he was working on a case like this. And especially this particular case. There was so much he had to do.

He finished writing his report about the bodies. They were in the morgue awaiting autopsy, but he had seen them before they were moved. Both had been in plastic bags, both nude and dismembered. Some articles of clothing had been thrown loose into the grave.

The urgency in Solomon's voice began to nag at him. He shouldn't have stopped to finish this, but if he didn't do it now, he wouldn't get a chance. He was reaching for his coat when all hell broke loose.

People started running in and out, and phones were ringing.

"What's going on?" he demanded from the coat rack.

"It's Redfield!" someone shouted.

"What happened?" *Redfield escaped*, he was thinking. *Damn it to hell, Redfield escaped.*

"He's dead."

"Huh?"

"Hanged himself."

"With what?"

"Tore up his shirt."

He couldn't believe it. How could this have happened. He wasn't finished yet.

There was so much to do still. So much, before the case was complete. It was getting him all churned up inside. Probably starting an ulcer.

A drink. He would go to Solomon's right away.

"I'm off duty," he announced and went out to his car.

18

*H*E needed her. He wouldn't let her leave.

"Make love to me," he had said. "I need you to make love to me."

What do *I* need? she wondered. But it hadn't mattered. His beautiful eyes had pleaded with her.

They had gone upstairs to his big double bed. They had kissed and embraced, but they hadn't made love. This time it was not she who had stopped him. She wondered if the drink had made him impotent.

He lay on his elbow, looking down at her. "I just need you here," he said again. "Do you know we have a lot in common?"

"Like what?"

"Well, for instance, I used to be in real estate, too."

She almost laughed. She scarcely considered it common ground. The office was not really a part of her.

"How come you never mentioned it?" she asked.

"It was a long time ago." He relaxed his arm and lay down on his back. "I liked it, actually. I liked going into houses, different houses. But there was a slump and I couldn't make any money so I took up law."

"Which do you like better?"

"I don't know. I like to help people."

"People like Bobby Redfield."

"He has a right to his day in court."

She supposed he did. "What's going to happen to him?"

"First they have to catch him. I don't know if they can."

"But I thought—" It had been in the newspaper and on the radio. She couldn't have imagined it.

"You're not really talking about Bobby Redfield, are you?" she asked cautiously.

"Why not? Why do you say that?" He sounded tired.

Then he seemed to reconsider. He added, "Guess I gave myself away. Always was a weak person."

"But—then—why is Redfield in jail?"

"He confessed."

"But that's dumb. Why?"

"Maybe he did it."

"You just said— Are we talking about two different people?"

"That's very possible."

"Well, whoever did it," she said, "it's obvious he's so sick they can't just send him to prison."

"How do you know?"

"You told me. You said there were others, and it

wasn't for the money. And you said—about the fantasies. The dead girls."

"That's the terrible part," said Neale. "If it's murder alone, I can handle that, but the rest..."

"You mean it wasn't just fantasies?"

"You guessed it."

"Please don't tell me about it. I don't want to know."

"How about another drink?"

She was not sure she could swallow at the moment, but he had already gotten out of bed. They dressed and went down to the kitchen. This time he mixed a shot of gin into her ginger ale.

"You didn't like that, huh?" he said as he pried loose a tray of ice cubes.

"What, the plain ginger ale? It was okay."

"What I was saying about—him."

"Oh. No."

"What do you think they should do with him?"

Those luminous eyes. They seemed frightening now.

"If he's sick," she said, "it's not his fault, but I just don't understand. I can't see why anybody'd even want to touch a dead body."

"That's the way it is. It's death. Sex and violence and death—they're all the same thing."

"But it's life. Sex is life." She shivered, remembering her fantasy of having a child with Neale.

"Maybe," she said, not knowing how many times she had already said it, "I ought to think about going home."

"What for? We didn't eat yet."

"I know, but I really ought to get back. I guess I can't ask you to drive me to my car, can I?"

"Wait a while. I'll take you in a while."

He pulled her close to him, massaging the back of her neck, and then led her into the living room.

"I don't think you'll be able to take me," she said. "I can call a taxi. Could I use your phone?"

He sat her down on the sofa next to him. There was a telephone on the end table to his right. She tried to reach for it, but he blocked her way.

"I told you, I need you here," he said. "I need somebody right now."

"But why?"

"Because I'll go nuts by myself."

She took a deep breath, closing her eyes. "Neale, I'm a married woman."

"You're afraid of me, aren't you?"

"I just—I—I don't know how to relate to people who have been drinking."

"The same way you relate to sober people."

"It doesn't work. Alcohol changes people."

"It certainly changes *him*," Neale said.

"H—how?"

"It loosens him up. Relaxes the inhibitions. That's all he is, a mass of control, trying to hold himself in. That's why they never caught him. Because it was all in his mind and they never knew about it. He just fantasized."

"That's no crime," she said. "Fantasizing. As long as he didn't do anything."

"He did. He did, but they never caught him. He followed a woman once. He followed her out to her car, and when she bent to unlock the door, he put his hands around her throat. He was afraid to let go. Afraid she'd turn around and see him, so he kept squeezing and shaking her. Then she slid down onto the sidewalk and he ran away."

She would play along with him. It was all she could do. Pretend he was still talking about Bobby Redfield.

"That was the first time?" she asked.

"The first time he acted on it. Because of the drink. He followed her out of a bar."

"Didn't anybody see him follow her?"

"For a while, he was afraid," Neale went on. "He was afraid they'd find out, but nobody ever said anything. It just blew over."

"Was she dead?"

"He wanted to go back and look, but he couldn't. They might see him. He was terrified. It horrified him that he could do a thing like that, and he might be caught."

Beads of moisture stood on his forehead. It was all so unreal. She couldn't believe how unreal it was.

"You're sweating," she said, "and it's cold in here."

He looked at her with eyes that seemed black in the lamplight.

"Yeah, well, I still haven't gotten over what I felt when he told me about it."

"Yes."

"It was the beginning, that night he came out of the bar. It was a kind of—metamorphosis. All that time he'd had a preoccupation with sex and violence.

It was in all the magazines, the films. He never thought there was anything wrong with it, dreaming about it. But that was the beginning. It was—"

He stopped. He held his mouth tightly closed, and again his eyes were moist.

Then he said, "It was as if—that first time—as if he sold his soul to the Devil."

She nodded. She was afraid to speak.

"Committed," Neale went on, "to that course of action. As if he sold his soul to the Devil. It gave him a kind of freedom. At first. And then later he wanted it back. His soul. He wanted it and he couldn't get it back."

She twisted her fingers and tried to think of something to say. Something to bring normality back to the room. Into the silence, the telephone rang.

She jumped. He stared at it, letting it ring a second time before he picked it up.

"Yes, that's right." He listened for a moment. "What?" And then again, "What?" She watched the blood drain from his face.

"That's terrible. Terrible. When did it happen?"

19

*W*HEN Mike arrived at the Thayer house, he saw Solomon's car, but not Libby's. He knew she should have been home hours ago.

It was several minutes before Solomon answered the doorbell. He looked as though he had been wakened from a deep sleep.

"What's up?" Mike asked.

"It's all happening at once."

"It sure is." One right on top of the other. First the two bodies, then Redfield kicking off.

Solomon led him into the study. That meant he was all business. Mike thought longingly of the drink he had hoped to have. At least he had packed a couple under his belt before he came.

He sat down on the couch, but did not take off his jacket.

"Libby working late?" he asked.

Solomon grunted irritably, then said, "I've been getting a lot of stuff. I keep seeing them, the two girls you found."

"Yeah?"

"He shot one. His usual M.O. is strangulation, but he likes guns. A passion for guns. He's sexually inadequate. A recurring problem. That's why he— They have to be dead or dying."

"Yeah," said Mike, "that kind of thing, it usually means a problem."

"He imagines a love scene, even when he's killing them."

"What did you see? Tell me."

"He shot her, in the woods up there where he buried her."

"Who, Basile?"

"No, one of the women you found today. The one underneath. He shot her in the chest."

"You're right. Son of a gun."

"She's on the ground, dying. I see her twisted, with one arm flung out. She makes a gurgling noise. Trying to breathe. He hears the sound. Hears her saying she loves him."

"She loves him, after *that?*"

"Not really. It was only a death rattle."

"I see."

"The man I'm talking about," Solomon went on, "seems perfectly normal on the surface, but it's only an illusion. He's not anything that he seems, even to himself. He believes the illusion."

"Yeah, I know. Bobby Redfield."

"Will you please indulge me? It's not Bobby Redfield. I don't know who it is. I never see his face."

"How come?"

"I think—" Solomon wasn't sure. He had never

had this problem before. "I think he's not there."

"What the hell does that mean?"

"To himself. He's not there. He doesn't see himself."

"You mean he's not real?"

"To himself. He's not real to himself."

"I don't get it," said Mike.

"He doesn't experience himself as a real person. That's jargon, but it's true. Hang on."

Mike hung on.

"It's dark," Solomon went on. "He's there, in the woods, crouching. By the grave. He came back."

"Back to the grave?"

"Came back to see it. He's digging, scraping away the dirt. He stops."

"What's he want?"

"To see if it really happened."

"He doesn't know if he did it?"

"Right," said Solomon. "Once it's over and he's had his—release, or whatever, the whole thing doesn't seem real. He can't believe it, and he can't accept it."

"How do you know all this?"

"Every now and then, when I see these things, I catch a glimpse of his feelings. But never his face. Never his identity. The only times I've seen him, he had a stocking mask on."

"You mean the guy in Knapp's apartment."

"And my visions. The mask is actual, but it's—it's the way he is, too."

"That doesn't make it any easier, Sol."

"I'm sorry. I only receive these visions. I don't produce and direct them."

"Yeah, I know. I know."

After the phone call, Neale settled back against the couch cushions. He seemed almost asleep, his hand resting on the arm of the sofa, his fingers lightly curled around his drink.

"It's over," he said. "Redfield."

"What do you mean?"

"Suicide."

"*Really?* But then—isn't that almost like a confession?"

"He already confessed. And it isn't. What it's like is, he was an addict. They get that way sometimes, if they don't have a fix."

"Oh. Well, is the case closed? Since he already confessed."

"I don't know if it's closed. They still don't have the girl."

They would go on looking for her, and Solomon would help them. Until they found her, or her body, the case would stay open. She wanted it closed.

"Okay," said Mike, "let's find the Basile girl, and that'll wrap it up. You told me you saw her a while ago."

"I saw her, but I still don't know where she is. I couldn't follow her. She was in the trunk of a car, and of course she didn't see where it was going."

"You need to follow the suspect," said Mike, who

by this time knew exactly how Solomon worked. "I brought a picture."

It was a full-face mug shot of Bobby Redfield. Solomon took the photograph and studied it.

He looked into Redfield's eyes, waiting for the images to appear. Instead, the screen in his mind remained blank, gray, like a television set turned off.

"Nothing?" Mike asked.

"Nothing. And you know why."

"He's dead."

"What?"

"Redfield knocked himself off this afternoon."

Solomon digested the news and then laid the picture aside.

"That's not it." Death had never stopped him before.

"Okay, what is it?"

"You know as well as I do. I told you Redfield isn't the man. His confession was false."

"Can't help it, Sol. It was the only lead we had."

"And now he's dead, and the killer's still out there. He got another one last night. I dreamed it."

"Yeah, you could be right about that. They reported a girl missing up near Wayne."

"Then how can you possibly think it's Redfield?"

"Just missing, is all. She could have run away, eloped, anything."

Solomon pressed his hands to his forehead. He still saw nothing, but he felt the cold. A bitter wind blowing from somewhere.

"She's outside now."

Mike looked shocked. "Who?"

"I don't know who, but I feel the wind. I feel—cold."

"So what's it mean?"

The screen was coming alive. He saw fingers running through long red hair.

Damn, he didn't need this. Not now. He tried to cancel it.

"You saw something?"

"My wife."

"What's she got to do with it?"

"Nothing, nothing. Wait, I see—it's a tree. It has no leaves."

"None of them have, right now," Mike contributed.

"A tree, and there are bushes."

He kept seeing that red hair. For a moment, his nose was filled with the smell of whiskey.

She was probably in a bar and he was fondling her hair.

He knew Mike had had a drink. Maybe all he smelled was Mike.

"Damn it," he said as the images shattered and disappeared. "I just can't get anything."

"Tomorrow?"

"I don't know."

"Don't worry about it, Sol." Mike's shoulders straightened as he stood up. "If it weren't for you, we'd be doing it on our own anyway."

"I keep feeling that cold. I *feel* it."

"But what does it mean?"

"I feel—as if—there's not much time."

He had wanted to stop working for the night and

relax. He couldn't get Libby out of his mind, but something else was battering at him. A terrible sense of urgency.

"Mike, she might be alive."

"Who?"

"The girl. Amy."

"Alive? How could she?"

"I feel that cold. I feel we have to hurry."

"But if you can't—"

"I've got to. No, wait. There's water. It's near water, but that hasn't anything to do with her. It's just there."

"Near water? With all the lakes and reservoirs we've got in Jersey? Not to mention the ocean."

"It's small water. There's something about it. Something that means something. And a hill."

"What are you doing?"

"Getting my coat. Let's go."

"Hey, man, I'm off—"

"Mike, listen to me. We're running out of time. If you want to save that girl's life, it's now or never."

20

"WHICH way?" asked Mike as they got into the car.

"The Basile house. I'll try to pick it up from there."

Solomon didn't have much hope. He kept seeing that long red hair, Libby's hair. He saw it wrapped around a man's hand.

"Hurry," he said as Mike stopped for a traffic light.

"You want me to run a light? This car isn't official, you know. It's mine."

"You can pull rank."

It wouldn't do any good to hurry. Unless he came up with better directions, there was no place to hurry to, but he still had the feeling that they must reach the girl right away.

They were coming to the northwest part of the city, where she lived. He opened his window and tried to breathe it in. He had tried everything else.

"Are you sure Redfield killed himself?" he asked.

"Why?"

"If he's not the kidnapper, I figure he must be in on it."

"We figure so, too," said Mike. "He had the money. We figure he *was* it."

"He must have had a reason for confessing."

"You think somebody knocked him off to keep his mouth shut, right?"

"I just wondered."

"He hanged himself," Mike explained. "Nobody could have got in his cell and done it for him."

He slowed when they reached the end of the road on which the Basiles lived.

"Want to go in?" he asked.

"No reason to. I just wanted to see what I could pick up. There should be something, a violent crime like that."

Solomon got out of the car. He walked down the driveway in the cold, quiet evening, looking up at the bare trees on either side of him. He had seen a tree, but it was none of these. It was bigger, with a wide, spreading top. Again something tickled the back of his mind.

The outside lights were on, but the house was dark. Probably visiting her husband in the hospital. He wondered how she could stay alone in that isolated house after what had happened.

He heard a rushing sound. He thought it was the wind, but when he looked around him, the trees were still. Then he realized that what he heard was a car.

Except for Mike's car, the road was empty, but Solomon could hear the sound of tires moving rapidly, as though they were on a highway.

Instinctively, he stood aside. He could see the car now as it entered the driveway, moving silently and darkly with its lights turned off. He saw it approach the house and stop, buried in deep shadows made by the trees.

A man got out. He wore a short dark jacket and dark pants. His features were blurred. A stocking mask.

The man watched and listened. When he was sure that all was quiet, he unlocked the trunk of his car and left it open. He listened again, then went around to the back of the house.

Solomon didn't move, but now he could see the man at the kitchen door, again listening. All around were trees and bushes. Unless someone was in the woods, there was no chance that he would be seen. A perfect place for a crime.

When the man had assured himself that there would be no alarm, he fumbled silently at the door.

A key. The man had a key. Solomon saw an array of doors. It was a key that could unlock many doors. He also understood that such a key was legitimate—unlocking empty houses, he saw dimly—but not when used this way.

The intruder slipped into the darkened kitchen and listened again. For him, it was a long, nerve-racking wait as he assessed the situation and his chances. He could hear the sound of the television upstairs.

He was starting out to the dining room when he heard her coming. Heard her bare feet on the stairs.

He ducked back into the kitchen entryway. Then he peered around the door jamb. In his hands were the white cloth and the bottle of chloroform.

And then came the scene Solomon had witnessed before: the girl opening the refrigerator, looking for a snack. The white cloth over her mouth and nose, her eyes wide with terror. He saw her slump, the cloth still pressed to her face.

The man picked her up and slung her over his shoulder. Solomon watched him carry her around the side of the house to his car. He heard the lid of the trunk slam closed.

While the man got into his car, Solomon hurried back to Mike.

"I've got it. I got the car."

"You got the car? What did it look like?"

"Couldn't see much. It was dark. Let's go!"

"Where?"

"Follow it."

"Isn't that the hard way?"

It was the only way. Solomon could not get a fix on the kidnapper's mind. It was as blurred as his face under the stocking mask.

"Turn right," he said as the other car slipped out of the dead end road. Its headlights went on and it picked up speed. Solomon could smell the chloroform.

The kidnapper's car screeched around a corner.

"Right," he said again.

The car slowed. Evidently its driver realized he mustn't call attention to himself. The chloroform was making Solomon's head swim. He fought to stay conscious. To keep the image of the car in sight. It started to blur. He felt that there were waves of fog on the road.

"Take that left," he said, pointing.

Mike cursed. He had to stop and back up.

"Got any oxygen?" Solomon asked.

"No, why?"

"The chloroform. It's knocking me out."

"It's all in your mind, Sol."

"I can't help it. Go faster, I'm losing it. There's fog."

"Just tell me where."

"Up there, where the road splits. Take the right."

"We're getting out of town."

"Do you want the girl, or don't you?"

"It's not my jurisdiction."

"We'll worry about that later. You know what to do."

"Nobody's ever going to believe this," Mike said, "chasing an imaginary car."

To Solomon, the car was not imaginary. It was an afterimage. He said nothing.

Again he saw the taillights disappear into fog. He saw the tree again, and bushes. That was no help at all.

They were tall bushes. He thought they might be overgrown privet. He needed an architectural feature, something specific.

He smelled dank concrete.

"We're losing him."

Mike increased his speed.

Solomon asked, "What would be underground?"

"Us, if we keep this up."

"It's a room. Some kind of room underground."

"Basement. Is that where she is?"

Solomon could not reply. Something struck the base of his neck, knocking him forward. The next moment, he felt as though his brain were on fire.

The sensation ended abruptly, and he fell back against the seat. When he looked ahead, the car had gone.

He put his hand to his neck where he had felt the pain.

"He shot her and left her for dead," he told Mike. "Can you speed up a little? I don't see it.

"We passed a road back there."

"Oh, hell."

"What do I do? Keep on or go back?"

"I don't know, Mike."

They were out in the open country. He must have been along this road before, but in the dark, it was unfamiliar.

"Pull over," he said. "I'll try to get something."

Mike pulled off onto the shoulder. "If he left her for dead, is she in the same place she was before?"

Solomon felt the wind again. He realized that what he had thought was a concrete smell was damp earth and rock. He felt something scratchy against his cheek.

"She's outside under a pile of leaves. She's dying."

"Hell, man, I'm doing the best I can."

"I know, I know."

He felt it again. He felt closed in, but not entirely. Wind was swirling the leaves above him.

"It's like a pocket of rock. He didn't have much time. There was no time to dig."

"Why?"

"Had to leave her. He—"

The red hair again. He saw Libby with her eyes closed. Her lips moved. He tried to see what she was saying.

"Well?" said Mike.

"Wait, it's Libby."

"Is she in trouble?"

He hadn't thought so. He wasn't sure.

She was trying to say something. He thought her mouth formed the word *help*.

21

"Do you know you have beautiful hair?" Neale asked.

"Yes, you told me."

She wished he hadn't told her. She wished Solomon had never mentioned anything about hair.

She wished none of this was happening.

"I like long hair," he said.

Probably she was making something out of nothing. Because of her guilt. That was it. Her guilt. It was killing her.

"Neale."

"Yes?"

"I really think I should be going. Before Solomon comes here."

"How would he know where you are?"

"He can do that. I told you."

"Every time?"

"Well..."

"Why don't you call him and tell him you're working late?" Neale suggested.

"Because if I were, I'd have called him long before now. He'll know something's up."

"Tell him you kept thinking you were going to finish your work and go home."

"It's after ten."

"Try it. Call him."

He picked up the telephone and handed it to her. "Call him."

"Neale—"

"Go on."

She dialed her home number and heard it ring. She held the receiver tensely, afraid he would answer. If only he wouldn't. If only she could hang up.

Six. Seven. Eight. She pressed the disconnect button and handed it back to him.

"There's no answer."

"You see?" he said, replacing the phone. "You have nothing to worry about."

"Maybe he's already out looking for me." She thought it more likely that he was in the shower.

"How much does he know?"

"He doesn't know anything. Only that I'm seeing somebody."

"You told him?"

"I was angry. I didn't tell him who you are."

"I hope not."

Again he leaned back and closed his eyes. She sat quietly, scarcely breathing. Maybe he would fall asleep. She could get out of there. Find a pay phone somewhere.

His hand was still wrapped loosely around the

whiskey glass. She saw his fingers relax. She held her breath, afraid the glass would fall and wake him. If she could just get it away from him. She started, very slowly, to rise.

The shift in her weight made him grunt and tighten his fingers around the glass. She was still half sitting on the couch. She did not dare move.

Gradually his breathing became slow and steady. His head rested on the sofa back and his mouth was open. Once more the fingers loosened. She waited.

He took in a breath that became a snore. She saw his eyelids flicker.

Another snore. She tried again to get up. It meant another shift of weight. After each shift she held her position until she was sure it had not disturbed him.

The snoring became steady. She was all the way up now. Her shoes were off and she moved silently to the other side of him. She took hold of the glass. He did not react. Gently she slipped it from his fingers.

She set it on the coffee table and picked up her shoes. If she could get out the door...

It would be better if she could use his telephone, but that might wake him. She listened to the snoring. It was heavy and rhythmic. With infinite caution, she picked up the phone and slid the directory out from under it.

She flipped through the yellow pages, looking for the *T*'s.

Taxicabs. Radio call. Twenty-four hours.

A penciled doodling on the opposite page caught her eye. She stared at it, gradually realizing what it was.

A disembodied arm. A leg.

Solomon, help me!

She didn't care what he would say. Didn't care about a lifetime of "I told you so's." He was safety.

She had to get out of there quickly, while Neale slept. Instead of the taxi service, she dialed her home number.

22

*T*HEY had pulled to the side of the road, where they sat studying a map. Mike held a flashlight while Solomon, with his finger raised above the paper, waited to be guided.

"I feel as if it's up here somewhere." He indicated an area vaguely north of them. "I'm not really getting much at all."

"Do you want to call it a night?" asked Mike.

"No, I still feel she might be alive."

"You think so?"

"I have a very strong feeling. I could be wrong."

He tried to make his head work. It felt as though it were stuffed with cotton.

"Point the way, then," said Mike.

"Maybe if we take this road..."

"Up here there's nothing."

"That's what we're looking for. Nothing."

They drove on into the black countryside. Solomon had no visions. The only thing that guided him was a hazy feeling of what felt right.

Solomon!

He looked up. That was odd. He thought he had heard her voice.

He decided it couldn't be, although his earlier vision, of the mouthed word *help*, disturbed him. She was out with her lover, he told himself, enjoying every minute. The sound of her voice must have been an imprint left from some other time.

"Wait!" he said.

Mike slammed on the brake. They had passed an intersection.

"Try that road to the right." Damn, that was dangerous, letting her distract him like that. He needed every nuance of feeling. He needed to evaluate. He would have to get her out of his mind altogether.

Mike backed up and made the turn.

"If she's in a pocket of rock under some leaves, how are you going to find her?" he asked.

"We'll just have to keep looking. I hope the batteries in your flashlight are good."

"They'll hold up better than I will. Do you know I didn't have dinner?"

"Look at it this way, Mike. What if we don't find her, and weeks later she turns up dead? How will you feel then?"

"You made your point. Which way?" It was another intersection.

"Stop again."

He was getting something. Almost. It was there, on the edge of his mind. Some kind of connection. He couldn't get it into focus.

"I keep seeing a tree."

"Any particular tree?" asked Mike.

"That's what I'm wondering."

Mike waited. He had driven onto a shoulder again and left the engine running. Solomon found himself listening to the engine noise instead of his feelings. It was irritating. Everything was getting to him.

To Mike, too. Mike's breathing was audible and he drummed on the steering wheel. Solomon sensed an enormous tension. Mike had been under a lot of pressure with this case.

The tree. He remembered a tree when he had searched for Ritchie Knapp. That tall, bare elm.

It couldn't be the same place. That was too crazy.

Or was it? His mind began to race. There had been the intruder in Iris's apartment. He thought it was the kidnapper. Didn't know why, he only felt it. Why would the kidnapper have been in—

"Tell me something, Mike."

"Yeah!" Mike jumped. A pretty strong reaction, Solomon thought. The man was turning into a basket case.

"These sex freaks," he said. "Don't they usually stick to one kind of victim?"

"What do you mean?"

"Say you have a guy who goes after young women. Teenagers. Anyhow, they're developed, if you know what I mean."

"Right."

"Would the same person go after a little kid? Or would that be a different kind of freak altogether?"

"Usually," said Mike.

"Specifically, a little boy. It seems so different."

"It is. Sometimes they change, though. They

reach a different stage in their sickness. Sometimes they go for what's available. But you're right, that is a big changeover. I doubt if it'd be the same person. Why?"

"It wasn't even a changeover. It was more an aberration, if it was anything."

"Can't tell. Everybody's different. Do you mind cluing me in?"

"I keep seeing a tree."

"Yeah, you said."

"It looks like the same one that was on that property where I found the Knapp kid."

"How can you tell one tree from all the other trees?" Mike asked.

"It's an elm. There aren't too many elms anymore. They had a disease."

"I think you're pushing, Sol."

"I think so, too. But that tree. It's more than just a similiar-looking tree. It's as if it means something."

"Worth a try," Mike said bleakly, as he put the car in gear and nosed out onto the road.

"It was an abandoned house," Solomon remembered.

"Out of my jurisdiction."

"I see that *R* again. And two brothers. There are two brothers."

"The Knapp kid?" Mike asked.

"No, not him. Slow down." Solomon peered into the darkness, watching for the white boulder.

His mind teemed with thoughts—not real impressions. He thought about Ritchie Knapp. They hadn't been able to tell much from the autopsy. It was possible that he had been left off somewhere near the house and then had fallen into the pond and drowned. Kids were usually attracted to water. But it was certain that he had been abducted. He was too far from home.

It happened all the time, little kids picked up and molested. There were too many disturbed people around. What was the connection with Amy Basile and the others?

Happened all the time. He remembered talking about it that night with Mike and Evelyn. He remembered Libby saying they were all men. He heard her voice.

Solomon, help me!

He couldn't think about that now. He had to find the girl before she died.

"There. Turn off there."

"Is that a road?" asked Mike.

"It is. It looks better in the daytime."

"It doesn't feel so great." They bounced into a pothole. Mike let out a few blue words.

Then he said, "She can't be alive. It's too cold."

"She won't be for long," Solomon answered.

"I can't go faster. I'll break an axle."

"Do you know anything about the people who own that house?"

"Yeah, we checked it. They're dead."

"Who pays the taxes?"

"A son. He doesn't live around here. I don't think they're a factor, Sol."

Libby had said they were all men.

"Where does he live?"

"Hell, I don't know. It's not my jurisdiction.

Where is this house of yours, anyway?"

"Keep going."

He wished he didn't have that feeling about Libby. He'd had it before and he couldn't get rid of it. Something about danger. But it couldn't be. It must have been the dissolution of their marriage that bothered him. That would give him a bad feeling, too.

"There, Mike, up ahead. That's the entrance."

"Son of a gun," said Mike as he pulled up to the two posts and stopped the car. "I wish it wasn't dark."

"We can't wait." Solomon opened the door. Mike followed with his flashlight.

"It's a desert," he said. "A real desert out here. I wonder why the guy never sold it."

"Probably a white elephant." Solomon waited for something to give him a sense of direction. All he felt was the cold and the searing pain at the back of his neck.

"Rocks," he said. "We have to find the rocks."

They started up the driveway. Mike said, "I don't see any rocks. It all looks flat to me."

"Not in back. It slopes down, but I don't remember any rocks like the ones I keep seeing."

The impressions were gone. Solomon felt only one thing, and that was Mike's skepticism. He tried to tune into the girl.

"Well?" asked Mike. After the heated car, they shivered in a cold breeze.

"I can't get anything right now."

"Maybe you're out of her range," Mike said sarcastically.

"She may be unconscious."

"You said you felt cold."

"That, too. I can feel cold because her body's cold, even if she's unconscious."

"Probably dead."

"Shut up, okay? I don't need that."

In the dim light, he saw Mike staring at him. Was it surprise? He hadn't meant to snap. For all of his adult life, ever since he outgrew his youthful insecurities, other people's doubts had been merely an annoyance, not a hindrance. Now it was different. He had failed too often lately.

"Sorry," Mike muttered.

They reached the house. Mike ran his flashlight over its facade, the tightly fastened door and the boarded windows.

"Rocks," said Solomon.

"We could use some better light than this."

Solomon looked up at the quarter moon. Even that was no help.

He tried telepathy. Tried calling to her and asking where she was.

In answer came that cry again. *Solomon. Help me!*

"I can't believe it," he said.

"What?"

"Libby. I keep hearing her."

"Maybe she's in trouble."

"I don't think so. We had a fight. I'm probably hearing reverberations."

"Yeah, I get a lot of those when me and Evelyn fight."

They started down the hill in back of the house.

"There's the pond." He pointed it out to Mike.

"You realize," said Mike, "if you could find that Knapp kid way out here, you haven't lost your touch."

"Did I say I had?"

"I think you got worried a few times. I think now the problem is there's nothing to pick up."

"She's here. She's got to be here."

"I don't see why. It's not where the others were found."

"I can't help it. I feel it."

Maybe he still felt Ritchie Knapp. He couldn't be sure.

"How about inside the house?" Mike turned his flashlight on its back windows, trying to see whether there could be a way in.

Solomon considered it. But he had felt dry leaves. She was buried under leaves.

He took another look around the garden. He saw no rock formation other than a decorative terraced effect of small stones. Maybe he was wrong. Maybe it was inside the house. The basement, perhaps.

He followed a jiggling beam from Mike's flashlight and found his friend prying away a loose window board.

Gradually she woke and thought she heard voices. They were doing it again, her grandmother and others, calling to her.

She hated waking. It made her feel the cold. She had never imagined that there could be such cold.

Somewhere above her she saw a light. She managed to turn her head.

It was only the moon. A little bit of a moon. She was outdoors. Cold.

Her throat hurt. She remembered his hands squeezing her throat. The roaring in her head.

And another memory. Only a glimpse. His eyes, dark and excited. She had blacked out. When she woke, she was outside. Frozen. Her hands and feet were tied. She couldn't understand how she got there, until she tried to swallow.

His eyes. He had *loved* killing her.

She couldn't move. She drifted in and out of blackness. Watched the moon recede and come back. When it came back, she was cold. So cold.

23

MIKE ran his flashlight over the room they had entered. It was empty and bleak. Chunks of plaster and peeling paint lay scattered on the parquet wood floor. A pair of French doors in the far wall led away into darkness. The cold inside the house was intense.

"Let's hope we don't go through the floor," Mike said as he took a step forward. "You coming? I'm going to look around down here and then upstairs. Unless you've got a better idea."

Solomon began to move about the room. He was feeling something, but he did not know what. Perhaps it was Ritchie Knapp's agony from a whole year ago.

"It's somewhere here," he reported.

"What is?"

"Where he kept her. It's someplace—dark. Someplace where light wouldn't show on the outside."

"The basement?"

"Let's try it."

Mike went through the French doors, with the

flashlight beam darting ahead of him. Solomon followed.

It should have been the reverse. Usually, in these searches, it was he who led the way. He felt ineffectual, useless. Frustrated. It was her fault. She had undermined him, damn her.

They crossed a short hallway and entered another large room. There were more French doors, and sour, musty smells. The wallpaper was streaked below a window, where rain had come in.

"I'll sell it to you cheap," said Mike. "It's a handyman's special."

"I'm not a handyman," Solomon answered.

He hadn't meant to damn her. When he thought about it, he felt a sharp pain in his gut. He wanted her back. That, if he were truly honest with himself, was what he really wanted.

He knew she would never come. It wasn't because of his age. That was a cop-out, he realized now. It was something in the way they related to each other, and now it was too late.

"Hey, over here."

Mike had found the kitchen. Attached to it was a walk-in pantry, and in the pantry was a door. Mike tried it and found it locked.

"Hell," he muttered. "Takes care of that."

"No, it doesn't," said Solomon.

"What, you've got a key or something?"

"No, just a pocketknife. Turn the light on those hinges, will you?"

"Sol, this is private property. You're not taking off the whole door!"

"When it's a girl's life, I am." Solomon chipped away layers of old paint to get at the hinge pins.

"I'm looking the other way," said Mike. "I was outside when you did this."

"Don't worry, we're not breaking anything. We can put the door back when we're finished."

"What makes you think there's anything down here, with the door locked tight? How could the kidnapper get down?"

"I couldn't tell you," Solomon replied. "But I was interested when you mentioned the name of the family that owns it. I keep seeing an *R*."

"Yeah, you told me. Maybe that refers to the place. The Randall place."

"Maybe."

He would have to see more than an *R*. After all his past successes now he only came up with zeroes. Maybe he had been too good in the past and had begun to expect too much of himself. Or maybe he was too full of himself now.

He pulled the pins out of the hinges and carefully lifted away the door.

A flight of steps led down into a void.

"After you," said Mike. "I'll light your way."

They descended into a small, concrete-walled area that contained the oil burner, various white humps that turned out to be sheeted furniture, a rusted blue bicycle, and a stack of shelves containing odds and ends and a box of empty glass jars.

In the righthand wall, the flashlight revealed a door covered with peeling brown paint. Mike went to open it. Solomon followed, grazing his shin in the dark. He patted the thing he had struck, feeling its shape. A rollaway cot with a loose bar. He saw the hitchhiker again, tied to a bed. A wave of terror, her terror.

It was even stronger, coming from the room Mike had found.

"Hey, Sol!"

The room was small and empty, a kind of bunker constructed of cinderblock.

"What do you make of it?" asked Mike. "Think it's supposed to be a fallout shelter, maybe?"

Solomon held his hands to his ears. He could feel it, the pain and the horror. He heard their cries howling around him like a wind.

"This is it," he managed to say.

"How can you tell?" Mike ran his flashlight over the walls. "There's nothing here. I think you're guessing, Sol. It's okay." He turned and started out of the room.

Solomon blocked the way. He was barely aware of Mike. He only knew what had happened in the room, all imprinted there. He saw her on the floor in her white nightgown.

"Sol, we're wasting time. There's nothing here."

"So close."

"It's okay, you made a mistake. Don't worry about it."

"No. No, I *feel* it."

"Look, friend, it's dark, we can't see anything anyway. I'll tell you what. Why don't I take you home, then I'll come back with the locals."

"You don't believe me, do you? I don't care about that, Mike, but a girl is dying."

"So what do you want to do? Want to try upstairs?"

She wasn't there, Solomon knew, as they started up the basement steps. The place was down here, where any light the man used would be hidden from outside.

Nevertheless, they searched the second floor, one empty bedroom after another. He heard the wind blowing through cracks, heard a shutter banging.

He heard voices crying for help. Libby's voice and another.

Libby.

He felt the wind, felt hands on his throat.

"I want to try the basement again," he said. Maybe it was only past distress that he felt there, but it seemed stronger than that. More immediate.

They went back down the basement steps. Mike began looking under the sheets that covered the furniture. Solomon was drawn back to the second room, but they had only one flashlight. He groped in the dark. He could almost see it. The man had used a gasoline lantern. He saw its light.

He turned from the room. She was killed there. Strangled. He didn't have time to dispose of the body. He carried it—carried it over here.

Solomon felt along the wall. He caught a spider web against his face and brushed it away with his sleeve.

His hand touched something. It felt like metal. A

rectangle. Something set in the wall. He felt a handle.

"Can you bring the light over here?" he asked.

"You found something?"

"A door. I feel there's something inside."

Mike came over with his flashlight and shone it on the wall. The door was about three feet high and three feet off the floor.

"Dumbwaiter shaft," he said. "You know what I'll bet you'd find if you opened that door? The dumbwaiter."

Solomon opened the door.

Inside, as Mike had predicted, was a heavy wood dumbwaiter and a double line of frayed rope.

The dumbwaiter rested slightly askew and seemed a little too high for its opening. Solomon pulled on one of the ropes, trying to lower it. Instead, it tilted farther.

He tried another rope. The dumbwaiter began to move. When it cleared the bottom of the opening, Mike shone the flashlight into the shaft.

"Well." His voice sounded strained. "There's your live one."

She was dead, all right. Solomon could not see much of her face, but he recognized her.

"That's the one," he said.

"It's not Basile."

"The one in my dream."

"So you found her."

He knew at once that she had been strangled, but in his mind he saw a gun. A handgun. A revolver. Then it was gone.

He felt as though a curtain had been pulled aside

for an instant, only long enough for him to know what was there. Now it had closed again.

"You're right," he said, turning from the dumbwaiter, "it's not Basile. We still have to find her."

"Hold on. We just found a body. There's a procedure here. I'll have to notify the locals."

"You pigheaded bureaucrat, to hell with your procedure. This girl can wait. Basile can't." Solomon felt his way toward the stairs.

Setting down his flashlight, Mike carefully closed and latched the dumbwaiter door. Solomon watched him test it to be sure it was secure. Then they went up to the kitchen.

"I don't get you, Sol," Mike complained as he placed the door back on its hinges. "If this one's dead, probably Basile is, too."

"It's always a possibility," Solomon replied.

"Where do you want to start? We already combed the house."

"I still think she's outside somewhere."

"There's an awful lot of outside."

Solomon returned to the window through which they had entered and climbed out. Even with the wind, the outside had a better feeling than the basement. It felt alive. He stood in the wind and tried to sense his direction.

He started down the sloping garden.

A rock garden. Rocks. Over there.

Down toward the pond where he had found Ritchie Knapp. He mustn't get confused. The energy was probably still there. It would always be there.

Mike came up behind him. "Got anything yet?"

"I keep feeling the pond. I don't know whether it's the Knapp kid, or what."

"Beats me how Bobby Redfield ever found this place," said Mike.

"Why not? It's here, isn't it?" Solomon did not bother to remind him that Bobby Redfield had been in jail when the girl they had just seen disappeared.

"I'm going down that way," he said. "I wish I'd brought my own flashlight."

Mike went with him, shining his flashlight on the ground ahead of them.

Obviously it wasn't Bobby Redfield. It was someone who knew the place. Someone connected with it.

They reached the pond. Mike shone his flashlight into the water.

Nothing was there. Even the crusts of ice were gone.

"So much for here," said Mike.

"It was this direction, not the pond itself. Can I use that for a second?"

Mike handed him the light. Solomon swept it over the hill that rose in back of the pond. He couldn't see very well. The light beam limited his range of vision. He gave it back to Mike and started up the hill.

It was coming strongly now. He could feel the wind again, and the leaves. He tried to separate it from the wind that he himself was feeling.

He heard voices calling. Voices of people who were known to her. People who had died. They were calling her. She hadn't much time.

He hurried on, hampered by the rocks and the clumps of grass. "Amy!"

Mike, stumbling after him, caught his arm. "Can the noise, will you?"

"What are you talking about? This place is deserted."

"He could return to the scene. We don't want to scare him off."

Mike was holding his arm, preventing him from running.

"So who do you think it is?" Solomon asked. "You told me Redfield's dead."

"Whoever. You don't want to scare him off."

"I want to find that girl. Either you come with me, or let me go."

Mike released his arm, and Solomon listened again.

He had lost it. Lost the voices. He called her in his mind.

It was Libby who answered. *Solomon! Help me!*

He concentrated on Amy. He saw the heart-shaped face, the long, dark hair. He saw a grove of wild plum trees.

It drew him diagonally up the hill.

And there, ahead of him, was a grove of small trees. Without leaves. Beyond them, he saw the rocks.

He turned back. Mike was standing below him, shining the flashlight up into Solomon's face.

The light blinded him. He continued on, blind. Something was about to happen. He had to find her first.

His vision was clearing by the time he reached the grove. He could see the formation of bedrock almost like a fortress against the side of the hill.

Low rocks. They could only hide a recumbent figure. Maybe nothing. He had to be right. A few more steps, and he leaned over the rock wall.

The leaves had blown off her face. She was very still. Probably dead. He brushed the leaves from her white nightgown and touched her foot. Ice cold.

A light beam bounced off the rocks. "We shouldn't have come here," Mike said.

Solomon turned to him. "Why don't you go and get the locals?"

"You're not the only one that gets feelings. I have a bad feeling about this. I'm sorry, Sol."

"It's okay. She's good and dead." Solomon felt it coming. He could only pray and hope.

"You're sure?"

"Right. So go and get the locals. I'll stay here."

"What for?"

"To make sure you don't lose your evidence. Okay?"

Solomon pictured a rough stone wall, a wall covered with moss and ferns and dripping water.

He turned back for another look at the girl.

He was still moving when the universe exploded.

Hot pain seared into the back of his neck. He thought he heard a voice.

Then nothing.

24

*N*EALE'S eyelids had fluttered at the sound of her dialing. She held her breath, afraid of when Solomon would answer and she would have to speak.

Solomon did not answer.

That meant he wasn't in the shower. He was out somewhere. She could get home before he knew. She waited until Neale was snoring steadily again and began to dial for a taxi.

The doorbell rang. She stopped, frozen. Neale stirred and rubbed at his face.

Whoever was there, it was *someone*. She set down the phone and went to answer the door.

A tall, blond young woman waited outside. She was slender and elegant in a white cashmere coat. Her eyes widened at the sight of Libby.

"Well, hello," she drawled. "Am I interrupting anything?"

"No," Libby answered huskily, "I was just leaving. He's asleep. He drank a lot. I—I'd like to get out of here before you wake him."

"Oh?" The woman stepped inside and closed the door. "Actually, I don't have to wake him. I just came to pick up something of mine. If I can find it, there's no problem."

Libby wished she would speak more softly. But at least she was here. Someone was here.

"If you mean—if you mean the nightgown, it's up in the bathroom."

Her eyebrows arched, concealing possible embarrassment, and the woman started upstairs.

Libby tiptoed into the living room for her shoes. Neale had stopped snoring. He seemed restless, but not quite awake. With the shoes in her hand, she hurried back to the hallway as the woman came down, stuffing something into her purse.

"I know this is ridiculous, but are you—could you give me a lift? Anywhere?"

"*Any*where?" the woman asked.

"It doesn't matter. I came with him in his car, so I don't have mine. I just want to get out of here."

"I could take you to a bus stop." The woman noticed Libby's wedding ring and smiled in private amusement.

"Anything." Libby slipped into her shoes and took her coat from the hall closet. "I can't tell you...He was just a friend. I didn't know he drank so much."

"Just a friend," the woman mocked as they went out to a new white Cutlass parked at the curb. "I know all about Neale and his friendships."

"Is he a little bit—strange?" Libby settled back against the seat. This person, she thought, knew Neale better than she did. Knew all about him.

"Very strange." The woman lit a cigarette. "He's

a lost lamb. Why, what did he do?"

"Nothing. He just seems—strange. He says odd things."

"Oh, really. Everybody you know makes sense all the time? Well, you're right. He is a little rough around the edges. I guess they had a pretty tough life, he and his brother."

"His brother?"

"You mean he didn't talk about it?"

"Well, he talked about—about—"

"You didn't get the same old broken record?" the woman asked in surprise. "The hysterical household, the uptight parents, the father deserting?"

"No, he just talked about Bobby Redfield. I think."

"He took that case, didn't he? Somebody ought to tell them. All that money, and he couldn't even finish law school. Did you know that? He's a phony, with phony credentials. Oh, well, it's not my problem. I'm finished with him."

"I don't blame you," said Libby.

The woman looked at her sharply. "Why?"

"Because he *is* strange, at least when he drinks."

"He's very dependent. I can't handle that. And no good at all in bed. Is this okay, the number three bus?"

"That's fine."

"You'll be all right?"

"Oh, yes." It was a well-lit corner. "Thanks so much. For everything."

Libby stood in the wind and watched the car drive away.

And then she remembered why the woman had

come. It was true, what Neale had said about the nightgown. It was true.

And the rest. Had he, after all, been talking about Bobby Redfield? Or—who? He knew so much about the killings. Who was it?

She waited a long time before the bus came into view. She boarded, slipped her coins into the slot, and sat down in welcome warmth. She wondered if Solomon was home yet. What would she tell him?

That her car wouldn't start. It was always a good excuse.

He would know, after what she had said to him that morning. He would probably throw her out, and then she would be alone. She didn't want to be alone, she wanted Solomon.

She walked the last two blocks to her house. None of the lights were on. He was not home. She would have to go in by herself to a dark, empty house.

Then she saw his car in the driveway. He *was* home. Maybe asleep. She walked faster, the sound of her heels echoing on the sidewalk.

She tried the door. It was locked. She dug in her purse for the key.

As soon as she was inside, she turned on a light. She looked in the kitchen, where she had found him the last time she came home to a dark house.

She looked in his study, and upstairs in the bedrooms, turning on lights all the way.

Perhaps he had left here. Maybe gone to that woman whose child he had found. But then he would have taken his car.

He could be out with Mike Tarasco. She thought

of calling Evelyn, but what if Evelyn said Mike was home? Then she would know he had left her.

She heard the sound of a car. It was stopping outside. She ran to the front door and looked through the window.

Mike Tarasco was getting out and coming up the walk. Before he could ring the bell, she opened the door.

"Oh, Mike! Do you know where Solomon is? I just got home, and he's not here. I had trouble with the car."

Mike came in and closed the door. He looked at her sadly. *An accident*, she thought. *There's been an accident.*

"Solomon's hurt," Mike told her.

She had been right.

And it was bad. His hands were shaking. He stuffed them into his pockets.

"Don't worry, it's not serious," he told her. "We were out together looking for that girl. He fell and hurt himself, but he's okay. I just thought I'd better let you know."

"Where is he?"

"I took him to the emergency room. He's going to call when he's ready. How about some coffee in the meantime?"

"Coffee?" She couldn't think. Coffee seemed irrelevant.

"I could use some. It's been a long day and I've got more work. Do you mind?"

"It's okay." She went out to the kitchen. Mike followed her. As soon as he had had his coffee, she would ask to be taken to the hospital where Solomon was. Or maybe she would drive herself there in Solomon's car.

She turned on the tap water and began to fill the glass carafe. She felt him close behind her.

She checked the water level and set the carafe on the warming plate. When she let go of it, Mike gripped her arm.

"He talked to you, didn't he?"

She stopped breathing. He held her just below the shoulder, so tightly she couldn't turn. Her mouth felt dry and useless.

"Who?" she managed to ask.

"Never mind. He talked to you. Dumb kid."

His hand clamped over her mouth. She fought it, kicking and twisting. She tried to scream. She was blacking out, smothering.

That horrible smell...

25

$\mathcal{S}$OLOMON felt himself waking. He was still only half conscious, lying on something hard and cold, feeling the chilly air.

The pain in his shoulder. Sickening pain.

It was *her* pain. He had known it hours ago. They would have to look outside for her.

As he became more aware, he began to wonder where he was.

Then he remembered. It all came back to him.

And he knew that the pain he felt was his own.

He had tried to be careful. He had tried from the moment they opened the dumbwaiter door. Something had slipped then. It was only for an instant, but long enough to show him.

In spite of his care, he must have given himself away. Or maybe it was only that he had gotten too close.

He would have to get out of here. He managed to pull himself to a sitting position. His head swam and a wave of nausea rose through him. He thought he was going to pass out again.

No way, he thought, looking down at the girl. She was very still, but he knew she was alive. He hadn't wanted Mike to know it.

Mike, his friend for all these years. How could Mike have kept it hidden?

He saw the man at the waterfall. Clearly. Powerfully.

And Mike.

Two brothers.

R.

Now he understood.

How? he wondered. How could it work out like that?

The pain was in his right shoulder. Gently he probed with his left hand. He felt the stickiness of blood. There was a lot of it, but not enough to kill him right away.

The thing that might kill him was exposure, as it had almost finished the girl.

He looked around at where they were. A dark hill in the middle of the night, the middle of nowhere. It was not a high hill. He couldn't see very far. He thought he saw a light, a single light, through the trees.

He tried to stand. The dizziness overcame him and he sat down again.

First he would have to do something about her. She was nearly dead. He would have to keep her going. He managed to bend over and shake her arm. Then he noticed that her hands and feet were tied.

"Amy! Can you hear me?"

She gave a faint moan. Barely a whisper.

"Hang in there, kid. I'm going to try to get help for you. For both of us. I'm going to get you back to your mom and dad."

The leaves rustled as she tried to move. He knew she was hurt. He didn't know how badly. The man had tried to choke her, but he never finished. He couldn't do his ritual. He had run out of time.

"Lie still," Solomon told her. "I'm going to give you my coat to keep you warm."

He unbuttoned his sheepskin jacket and painfully slipped his good arm out of the sleeve. It pulled on the wound. He gritted his teeth and tried to imagine himself whole, his skin unbroken. It helped a little. He worked the jacket off his injured shoulder and down the arm. Then he laid it over her.

"Keep you warm," he said. "You're warm now, Amy."

The power of suggestion. It would be good for both of them.

As he bent over her, he heard a scream.

He raised his head. It was Libby. In trouble.

He had to get out of there. He thought of leaving the girl and walking for help.

No use. It was too far. He'd never make it.

He'd have to get them here, somehow. Get help to come here. But how?

He knew a couple of other people who were psychic. Maybe a telepathic message.

There wasn't any time. He could go into shock. Without his coat, he would die. The girl would die, and Libby, too.

Libby. He had to get to Libby.

He tried to tune in to her. All he felt was pain and fear.

Another gust of wind blew, rippling the grasses.

Those dry grasses...

He wondered how far away that light was. He wondered if they could see. If they *would* see.

He checked the wind direction. The best place was this hill, but the girl was here. Her neck might be injured. If he moved her, he could kill her. He bent over her and felt in the pocket of his jacket.

Then he looked up at the top of the hill. It was only a few yards away. He could make it. The wind was blowing across the top, not down here toward the rocks. He would have to take a chance. He couldn't think of anything else.

"Hang on," he told her again. "I'm going to signal for help. I'll be right back. You stay warm."

He started up and clutched one of the plum trees for support. Only a few yards. He took another step.

Damn it, man, he told himself, it's only a shoulder wound.

He thought of Libby, and it got him to the top of the hill.

He was disconcerted to find that the ground was rockier here, but it was not completely bare. Just down over the side was a sparse patch of grass.

He felt the wind again. It seemed to gust in all directions. He'd have to be prepared. They might need to get out in a hurry.

Now for the old book of matches he had taken from his jacket. He opened it. Only five were left. Hardly worth carrying around, but he was glad he had. His head was beginning to feel light again.

He took out a match and struck it.

He struck again. Nothing. It had been in his pocket too long. Probably damp, or rubbed bare.

He tried another. Again nothing.

He struck a third.

It ignited. Almost immediately, the wind blew it out. Only two remained.

He lay down on the ground, forming a shield with his body. The pain made him dizzy.

He breathed hard, gasping for oxygen. He tried again to see his shoulder as whole.

It wasn't. Instead, he heard Libby calling him.

He struck the next to last match and touched it to a stalk of grass. Quickly he fed the tiny flame with more grass. As it flared, he moved back. And back again.

Another clump caught fire.

The wind gusted again. The blaze was spreading from one clump of dry grass to the next. Spreading down the hill. They would have to see it now, whoever they were. He looked toward the light he had noticed earlier.

It was gone.

Perhaps it had only been a car.

26

*S*OLOMON, *help me!*

She was suffocating in the trunk of his car. Some of the tape covered her nose. She couldn't breathe.

She remembered finding herself helpless on the floor, with tape over her mouth, while he tied her hands and feet. Then he had gone out to back his car into the driveway. She had dreamed, briefly, of freeing herself while he was out. The ropes cut too tightly, and then he was back.

Solomon!

Something jolted the car.

The door. He had closed the door.

She heard a roar as he turned on the engine.

Solomon! She tried to kick her feet. To scream. Anything. She would burst from the panic, the helplessness.

Suddenly she relaxed. Her panic flowed away as the car began to move. She waited, ready to feel which way they went.

Down the driveway. Only a few feet. She felt him hesitate. Then to the right.

She felt the turn all through her body. She concentrated. *Solomon.*

She would have to keep it up no matter how fast they went. Had to follow the distance and the direction.

Her concentration flagged. She thought Solomon was dead. How else would Mike have dared come to the house?

He isn't dead. He's alive. Solomon's alive.

The traffic light two blocks away. He had stopped. Then she felt the car turn left.

Where? How long could she last?

He would kill her. That was what he meant to do. Kill her, and then...

It didn't matter what happened to her afterward. She would be dead.

She didn't want to be dead. She sobbed, but it only tore at her throat. She couldn't take in air because of the tape on her mouth.

Solomon heard her voice, a high, thin wail. A wail like a—

Siren.

They were coming. Thank God. His folks were still inside the apartment. They hadn't believed him. Told him he was crazy. He didn't want them to die.

The siren grew louder. He shook his head, trying to clear it. He felt the heat from the fire.

God, the girl. He checked down the hillside. About six feet, he thought. Six feet away from her. He tried to make himself move.

He had to move. Had to do something. He was responsible. No longer eight years old. That had been forty years ago, that time they had the fire in his parents' apartment building. He had said it would happen, and no one believed him.

Solomon, help me!

He had to get to her. Had to do something.

He should have warned her. Should have known, but he couldn't. They had hidden it too well. He had failed.

Mike had had the advantage. He knew all about it. He also knew what Solomon could do, and what he couldn't. Mike had gone along, playing his game—except that it wasn't a game. Mike felt it was the most important thing he had ever done.

The siren came closer. It really was a siren. He saw red flashing lights.

He looked down. The fire was closing in on her. He tried to move.

She mustn't cry. It would kill her. Took too much air, and she couldn't breathe.

There had been more stops. Then another right turn.

What would he do? He couldn't take her to his house. Evelyn was there. And the boys. Did they know?

Solomon was dead.

They were moving along with no more stops, no turns. Out of the city. Where?

He'll never find me.

Out of the city, she told him. I know, because there aren't any traffic lights.

She tried to picture the direction. From the turns, she thought it must be north.

That was where Neale lived.

His brother!

If Neale knew what was happening, would he still cry for his brother?

More than for her. He didn't love her. And she had given up Solomon for him.

So terribly, terribly sorry. I love you. I really do.

He would never find her. He was dead. He had probably discovered Mike's secret, and this was Mike's revenge.

Solomon crawled down the hillside toward the pocket of rocks. He had to get her out.

Suddenly they were all around him. He could not believe they were real. Again he thought he was eight years old.

He pointed toward the rocks.

"There's a girl there. She's hurt. Be careful. Her neck is hurt."

"Looks like you ran into some trouble yourself," said one of the men. Solomon could feel the blood on his shirt. He felt the chill of the wind.

"Got to get out of here," he said. "My wife—"

"We'll get you out," they told him. "We'll get the police, an ambulance, the works."

Good. The police.

They set to work beating out the fire. Someone found the girl and ran back toward the house.

"Get the police," Solomon said. "Now. Urgent."

"They're on their way," he was assured.

"My wife—wife is in danger. Got to call the Fairmont Park police."

"Take it easy, fella. We've got a fire here."

"*Now!*"

"Mister, you'll have to wait till we put it out."

Couldn't breathe. What little air she could get smelled of the car trunk, and it choked her. She was battered from the ride. The trunk was filled with rigid objects, tools, and pebbles.

Mike. Always their friend. Only the other night, she and Solomon had cooked dinner for them.

The car slowed. She felt it veer to the right.

He would never find her. He was dead.

Even if he happened to be alive, he would never find her in time. If Mike had left the long road, it must have meant he was getting somewhere. He would do it soon. Take her out and kill her. Strangle her.

She began to cry again.

"Got to get," Solomon gasped, "police."

"Here's the police," someone said.

State police. Thank God.

"I'm Solomon Thayer," he told the trooper. "I work with the Fairmont Park police. The girl—" He pointed toward the stretcher that was being carried down the hill. "Amy Basile. Kidnapped. Now they have my wife."

"Wait a minute, mister, let's try it again slower."

"No *time!*" How to make them understand? They thought he must have strangled the girl. They were going to question him.

"Why the hell," he asked, "do you think I made the fire? Had to get you over here. I couldn't walk. He shot me."

"Who shot you?"

"Mike Tarasco."

"Detective?"

"Right. Oh, hell, my wife. He's got my wife."

A long road north. They were coming.

He put his hands to his head. "They won't stop." He would see the engines. Wouldn't come in here.

"Where's your wife?" asked the trooper.

"In the trunk of his car."

"Whose car?"

"Damn it. Tarasco. Find his car. He's going to kill her."

"How do you know that?"

"I—just—know. He's—"

They would never believe him. Not about Mike. He scarcely believed it himself.

"Let's go." He began to stumble down the hill toward the house.

"Wait a minute, mister. We've got a lot more—"

"Do you guys understand? He's going to kill my wife!"

He couldn't get through to them. Maddening stubbornness when he wanted them to listen. Was that how he seemed to Libby?

No more chance. No chance to make it up.

A rough road. The car slammed and bounced. She was shaken, bruised. Her head hit something knobby.

Please, she thought. Please get it over with.

Whatever happened, she couldn't go on like this. Another jolt. He must have put on the brakes. They were barely moving.

The car stopped and began to back up.

Solomon, help me!

"She's near here," he said.

"Where near here?"

"I don't know, but I can find her."

"If you don't know where she is, how can you—"

"Please believe me. It's her *life*."

Grudgingly they let him into the car. He told them he had to sit in front. One trooper drove while another rode in the back, watching Solomon.

"They're there," he said, pointing. "He started to come in here and then he saw the trucks. He backed away."

"How do you know all that?"

"Believe me. Please. I just do."

They drove down the road the way they had come in.

"Please hurry," said Solomon.

"Can't go any faster on this surface."

They reached the intersection.

"Take the right here," he said. "They went right. And I have to warn you, he's armed."

"Sure. He's a cop."

The trooper in back muttered something about stresses.

"It's not that," Solomon replied. "It's a family thing. Down that road there."

"Listen, just tell us where he is," said the driver.

"I don't know. I can only tell you where he went. He was heading for the Randall place. Saw the trucks."

He waited for another signal. Waited.

He wondered if she could be dead.

The car had stopped. He turned off the engine. This was it.

She whimpered and struggled against her ropes. It was happening. She couldn't believe it was happening.

Would he strangle her, like the others? Cut her up like the others? She remembered the drawings in the phone book. Something heaved inside her.

No dinner. She hadn't had dinner. Only the drink. Why hadn't she passed out like Neale?

She called to him. *Neale.*

No good. He was weak. Passed out.

The car shifted slightly. He was getting out. He would unlock the trunk.

He's going to kill me. Going to kill me.

Neale!

"Which way?" asked the driver.

He waited, hoping to feel something. He was drawn to the left.

"I think it's the left."

N.J. They had both been adopted later on. The initials were all he saw, but he knew it was the man at the waterfall.

Mike's brother. He was the one. Mike used his office to cover it up. He had to call in Solomon because he always did, couldn't do anything differently, but he blocked the truth.

Now he had her. She would know, because of the brother. It made her dangerous. And Mike was too far gone, too torn apart, to think of anything but pursuing the course he had set.

He waited for the feeling to come again. It had to come. His shoulder was throbbing. He felt weak. He had nothing but adrenaline to keep him going.

"That way," he said.

His right arm had tried to point. Pain ripped through his shoulder.

"A diamond. A big—earth—diamond. Is there a baseball field? Picnic ground?"

"Yeah, the town park."

"There's a white building."

"Several."

"It's locked."

"The toilet?"

"I see a tractor. Tractor mower."

"The maintenance building. How'd he get in?"

"He's not in."

"You ready to go on this?"

"I am, but keep it quiet. He's armed."

The car picked up speed. He saw lights flash by. A tavern. Ahead of them was a large, dark area. He knew it was the park.

She heard his key in the lock. She took several deep breaths and let her body go limp.

He opened the lid. She felt the air on her face and hands. She felt bruised.

Resisting the impulse to gulp fresh air, she breathed shallowly and evenly. He started to lift her out.

"Damn it, I'm sorry," he said.

Let him think she was unconscious. It might slow him down. He would have to wake her before he could enjoy killing her.

He pulled her upright. She forced herself to stay limp and let her head fall forward.

He held her for a moment. A long moment. What if he dropped her? She couldn't catch herself as she fell back into the trunk, on top of the jack and the other tools.

He seemed to be listening. Then she heard it, too. It sounded like a car.

He muttered angrily. Then he let her go. She fell, striking her head on something hard.

She had done it. There was a stifling thump as he closed the lid.

The car rocked. He had gotten in. She waited for the door to slam.

Instead she heard voices. Only a little, through the trunk. She couldn't hear their words.

Voices. Someone had come.

If she screamed, he would kill her. If she didn't scream, he would kill her anyway. She tried to take a breath. She would never be able to make enough noise with the tape on her mouth.

Scream, she told herself.

A gunshot exploded.

She screamed. A muffled wail.

More gunshots, from farther away.

She lay cowering, waiting for a bullet to crash through the trunk. Waited until suddenly there were no more shots.

Instead, voices.

Someone was unlocking the trunk. *Please, not Mike.*

"She's in here," said a voice.

She opened her eyes. She had never seen anything so beautiful in her life. A state trooper.

"I was wrong," said Solomon as they were driven home.

Her mouth stung from the tape. "So was I."

He slumped against her, favoring his shoulder. It was bandaged now and the bullet had been removed. He wore a sling to ease the strain.

"I don't mean about Mike," he said. "I mean everything."

"So do I. And I—I—"

"I never guessed the man was his brother. And Mike—I don't think he knew. Not till the Basile case."

"I thought it *was* Mike. I mean after. But before—"

"I don't think he would have hurt you. The brother. It's usually strangers, someone who's not real to them. But Mike thought he must have told you too much. Mike was frantic by then. He wanted to make it look like the others, the other killings, and then cover up the whole thing."

"Maybe Mike's a little unstable, too," she said.

"Could be. He told me years ago that his parents were pretty high strung. Probably he and his brother felt like two against the world."

"I wouldn't be surprised," Libby said. "Especially—they put his brother in a home. They couldn't handle him. Just dumped him out of the household."

"He told you that?"

"Well, he told me it was someone else. Maybe Mike felt guilty, like survivor guilt. He didn't want anything else to happen. And when he found out about the killings— It's sad, you know, Solomon? Last week, Neale talked about his life as if it were normal. He invented a whole happy life for himself. It's really sad."

"It is," Solomon agreed, "for a lot of people."

"Where were you tonight?"

"Out in Roscoe. Where he took you."

"That was Roscoe? That's where—"

"I know. The childhood home of the Randall brothers. That's what they used to be, Neale and Mike. We found the Basile girl. Your friend left her there for dead."

"Is she?"

"No. She'll make it. There were a lot of others, though."

"What's going to happen to Mike?"

"He'll be buried."

"You didn't tell me."

"It's hard," said Solomon. "Hard to face. I think, at that point, it's what he wanted."

After a while, she said, "You were pretty close to Mike. How come you didn't know?"

"He didn't want me to."

"It isn't always that easy."

"I know it isn't. Part of it was the nature of his brother's illness. They were close enough so Mike could fall into that pattern of thinking, too."

"What do you mean?"

"A person like your friend," he explained, "is capable of thinking on two levels. He knows what he is, and he denies what he is. He has to, for his own protection."

"From what?"

"The truth. The horrible, dark inner person. He can't accept it. Can't accept himself for what he is, so he convinces himself he's not that. He even managed to attribute his crimes to someone else. Found the perfect patsy. Mike helped on that. They probably got him to cooperate by feeding him drugs."

She thought of Evelyn, and how it was going to be for her now. She tried to imagine.

"Solomon, I do love you."

He squeezed her tightly with his good arm. "It looks as if I had somewhat of the same thing. I just didn't carry it to extremes."

"What do you mean?"

"My insecurity. I guess I never really got over the way I felt when I was a kid and they didn't believe me. I took it out on you."

"And I—I did bad things, too, because of the way I felt about myself. I didn't mean it, what I said. I'm really sorry about all that. Really."

"And I'm sorry about Mike."

"Solomon, you *are* special. Never mind what people said to you a million years ago."

"Please, it's not that bad. It's only forty."

"I said it on purpose," she told him as she nuzzled his hair. "It might as well be a million, because it doesn't matter. This is now."